Intentionally
Blank

Intentionally
Blank

Buried Before
DEATH

A Novel

Fidelis F. Chiaboh

Miraclaire
Publishing

First Published in 2022
Miraclaire Publishing
Kansas City, MO 64133, USA
www.miraclairepublishing.com / info@miraclairepublishing.com

ISBN: 978-1-954154-13-1
© 2022 Miraclaire Publishing & Fidelis F. Chiaboh

Printed in the United States of America

Dedication

To

John Nkemngong Nkengasong

Chapter One

"Do our people not say that the old look after the child to grow its teeth and the child in turn looks after the old when they lose their teeth? Who will look after me when I lose my teeth?" Ayongnabobo Bam asked after a long moment of reflection as he struggled to get out of his bed early that morning. His heart was heavy and his feet slow to carry his body out of bed. He needed to get out of it as soon as possible because he had learnt right from the time he was a little boy that rising early made the road shorter. He struggled and struggled and in the end succeeded in raising only the upper section of his being and felt some numbness in his feet as they refused to move but only rested on the same spot like pieces of dry wood waiting for a dutiful son to split for his mother to use in preparing corn fufu for the family.

Early that morning, those who were still indoors could clearly hear the morning breeze as it murmured from outside. In every house, there was some amount of light. In some houses, it was the light and warmth from flames of fire burning on the hearths while in the others was simply the light of daybreak. It either invitingly entered through the opened doors or stubbornly trespassed through the cracks of the doors that were yet to be opened. The lord of the compound had unusually stayed longer in bed that morning and it was only the light stealing through the door cracks that was forcing him out.

"This is a bad sign. Is this how old I have become? Do I now need so much effort to move my legs? Maybe it is just the weight of the night on me" He said and then moved them with more than usual effort. Within a few minutes, they were hanging from the bed and he expected them to, as usual, unmistakably land on his sandals. For as long as he could remember, his feet, even in pitch-darkness, never missed his sandals. He knew that they knew the smell of those sandals and they knew he was aware of that and trusted in their ability to find those shoes for him. They were betraying him for the first time as it took him more than usual effort for them to find the old leather sandals he had used for a couple of decades. His first two attempts to place his feet on them were unsuccessful. This was strange to him and he wondered if it was strange too to his feet and even to those sandals carelessly lying on the floor in front of his bed.

He could partly guess what was bothering him. Seven long years had passed since he and his family buried their first son who had lost his life in a road accident in Adnemada town on his way to the nation's political capital, Ednuoaya, but it still looked to them as though it had only been yesterday that they suffered the loss of their son. Ayongnabobo Bam thought of his late son at all times but felt the pain of the loss even more whenever someone called him *Bo Bam*. He answered reluctantly to the greetings before complaining but making sure his interlocutor wasn't hearing.

"They call me Bo Bam after having eaten the Bam," he would say to himself.

It was in the habit of the people of Huba to address elderly people by attaching the name of their first or well known child to their name rather than just call them by names. This was considered a sign of respect and even those who had no biological children were either called *Bo* or *Na* because it was strongly believed by all villagers that once a child was born, it became the child of the entire village and not just that of its biological parents. It was a common thing to hear someone refer to an elderly man as *Bo Tim* and to an elderly woman as *Na Tim* which meant *Father of Tim* and *Mother of Tim* respectively. Whenever Ayongnabobo Bam was addressed as *Bo Bam*, his wrinkled face darkened and his eyes turned red. It always took him lots of manly effort to hold back his tears during such moments. After all, it was believed and said that " a man's tears flew into his stomach and not down his cheeks like a woman's"

2

Some old men in the village noticed the pain and bitterness in him whenever he was called *Bo* Bam and decided to tactfully avoid addressing him using his late son's name – and henceforth referred to him as *Nyindô Ngàm*, meaning Ngam's successor, since he was the successor to his maternal uncle, *Nchindô Ngàm* who died a blind man at 104. *Nyindô Ngàm* now took care of his own compound, four wives and many children before the burden of taking care of *Nchindô Ngàm's* compound, two wives and a few children. The load was heavy on him but the gods had always given him the strength to cope with all the responsibilities especially when his late son had been there to help organise the families. Things had been moving on well until the day news came to him that Bam had died in a road accident.

The entire family never stopped wondering and asking why death was so wicked to them that it had to take away the only ripe fruit of the basket. The day Bam died was the same day Nyindô *Ngàm* swore to neither forgive nor visit the land's seer, *Bo Finyah* ever again. He believed that *Bo Finyah* had deceived him by prophesying that his son, Bam, would live to bury him as was expected of every son. "Why did death have to single out and take away only the ripe fruit from my basket of fruits?" Bo Bam would ask whenever any of his children behaved waywardly.

He had always known that Bam was the light that was to show him way when he became old and probably blind. Bam was the stick with which he hoped to support his ailing self when the time came, the umbrella that was to cover him from sun and rain. He was the one who was going to fire gunshots and slaughter many goats at his funeral. He had admired Bam's industriousness and had assured himself that he was going to be an appropriate replacement when he would have left for the world beyond.

"Bam, when I go, mobilize your siblings to give me a befitting burial. When I join my ancestors I want you to fire guns such that death itself would be envious of me. I want you to pour libation and offer sacrifice to your ancestors like no one before you has ever done," this is what he used to tell Bam when he was still alive. Now

3

that he was no more alive many things had changed and all that change was towards the negative direction. It was the type of change that no one desired.

"If only Bam were alive! If only he were alive to split my firewood and fetch me potable water! If only my son were alive to beat some sense into your coconut heads for me!" One of *Nyindô Ngàm's* wives would say whenever she realised she had neither firewood to cook with nor water to bath with while her sons were playing around unconcerned about her wellbeing.

For the past seven years, Nih, Bo Bam's first wife and mother to Bam, had become completely empty of happiness and hope. She was never going to get over the tragic death of her son. She knew that the death of the only son the gods had given her was a marker of the beginning of her end on this earth.

"Were they not witches and wizards that ate up my only son?" she would ask anyone who had the concern and the patience to listen to the story of her son's death which she had narrated tirelessly as long as there were people she could speak to. This stopped them from visiting her because whenever their discussions concerned the death of her son, she ended up accusing everyone of being a part of that wizardry that wished the evil to befall her and would go ahead to lament that people were secretly making a mockery of her situation. There were times she refused to believe that her son was dead and gone. During such moments, she kept hoping that one day she would hear a different and favourable story about him.

For various reasons, it hadn't been a peaceful night in Bo Bam's compound. That was why he woke up with a troubled mind. The barking of dogs, croaking of frogs, mewing of cats and whistling of owls had made the night so dreadful to Bo Bam's household. Bo Bam himself who was a husband to six wives and a father to forty-seven children and a god to them all, had been worried all night. As the head of the family, only he had had the courage to go out in the darkest part of the night to address the evil spirit that was lurking in the darkness. When he could no longer bear the harsh wind that was threatening to take off the roof of his house; the wild barking of dogs, the dreadful hooting of owls and the shadows parading the compound, he got off his bed and went out to confront whoever was causing such disorder in his compound. When he first opened the door to go out, he got frightened and thought of closing it and going back to bed. What gave him courage to continue was the fact that it was his compound and he needed to impose his authority against whatever spirit that was lurking about.

'How can I fold my arms in my own compound and allow strange spirits to take control over it? Are we not suffering in Africa today because the black man folded his arms and allowed the red man to come and control him and his resources and soon became a master in his land?' he thought to himself before finally stepping over the threshold.

As he stood outside in the awful darkness, he beat his feet on the ground three times, took some earth from under his feet, spat on it and threw it over his head saying: "My hands are clean. Whether you have come to give or take go back because I do not have anything to give and I do not want to take. Go back to wherever you came from and say you didn't see me or any member of my family. Do not bewitch me or any member of my household".

Then he returned to his house and the frightful noises went dead for the rest of the night. The thoughts of his late son came to his mind as he lay in bed thinking and speaking to the vacuum for the rest of the night. It was in the early hours of the morning that some life returned to the whole compound.

The routine battle between darkness and light had just come to an end. This time, dawn had just defeated darkness and had sent him to where he would stay till he mustered enough courage and strength to return in the evening and try to revenge and maybe momentarily conquer dawn too.

It was the custom of the people to wake their children at the early hours of the morning so that they go outside for birds to fly over them. Whether it was only a trick to make the little ones wake up early or not, no one could say with certainty, but it was generally said by all and believed by some, that it was a good sign for the early risers for the birds to fly pass over someone's head and that when this happened, it was an indication that the gods were watching over them. Those natives who strongly believed in this philosophy became very happy if a bird, on flying pass over them, deposited its droppings on their heads. They would gladly say that that day was a lucky one and would go ahead to link every happy event of the day to the bird incident.

On the other hand, it was generally considered a bad omen for someone to open their door early in the morning and the first thing they saw was a black cat, an owl, a person suspected of practising destructive witchcraft or a creditor. Natives would do anything, if at all there was anything to be done, in order to avoid having to face any of these situations in the morning. However, if such a thing unavoidably happened, one would be expected to beat their feet on the ground three times, carry some earth where they stood, spit on it and throw it over their head saying: "My hands are clean. Go back to wherever you came from and say you didn't see me. Do not bewitch me". It was believed that after doing so the powers of evil were weakened and the innocents protected by the power of the earth from which all beings came and to which all shall return in death.

The doors to four of the five houses in Bo Bam's compound were already opened and the kids and fowls had come out of the houses and were going about their various businesses. Of the seven children who could be spotted outside; three of them, the older ones, were sweeping portions of the yard while the other four, the younger ones noisily yawned repeatedly and freely stretched out their arms. The many fowls went about their routine business: the mother hens croaking an invitation to the chicks and the chicks scrambling over ants and the pieces of food they could find on the ground. The cocks croaking courtship invitations to the hens and when the hens came close enough, the cocks climbed on their backs and stayed there briefly before dropping again. From their behaviour, one could notice that all hens were wives to the strongest cock in the compound and none of the hens appeared jealous of it. Jam, one of Bam's younger brothers, stood there watching carefully and wondering if all fowls were of the same race.

Maybe the agric fowls are of a different race and culture, but will they be so daring and primitive enough to impose their way of life on this breed of fowls? Has no foreign fowl preacher, probably from America, Britain or France ever come to Africa to preach to these fowls about heaven? To give them the Ten Commandments, tell them that polygamy is a sin and present to them New Rights which allow men to marry men, women to marry women and humans to marry animals? That is how the red human species came here and destroyed our African Religion by projecting it as being inferior and barbaric. Thereby presenting theirs as being superior and civilised,' he thought envying the freedom and happiness fowls and animals enjoy.

Three of Ndim's hunting dogs were happily wagging their tails in celebration to the fact that it was daybreak at last. The night had been evil! Ghosts, witches and wizards had paraded the compound like never before and they had had to bark all through until the early hours of the morning when the evil apparitions had returned to the dark regions of the earth probably waiting for night to return for them to resurface and rob the world of its love and peace by hunting victims to devour.

***

Nyindô Ngàm was still in his house pondering over the happenings of the previous night. True, he had sworn, on the day news came to him that his son had died, that on no occasion was he ever going to visit *Bo Finyah* for consultation, protection or for any reason at all. He couldn't understand why his son was leaving the village to his death and his own old-time friend and revered seer of the land would tell him that although the path was rough the gods had cleared the big obstacles and that his son, Bam, would live to bury him. As things were at the moment, it looked as though

7

Nyindô Ngàm had to go back on his words and visit once more, the eye of the gods to know if he had anything to say about last night's upheaval. After making up his mind, he asked his children to catch one of his black cocks. When they caught and put it in a bamboo splinter basket, he took it along talking to no one about where he was going but only told his first wife that he wasn't going to be long.

'We do not suffer illness when the doctor is around.' He told himself and marched out of the compound.

In slightly over forty minutes, *Nyindô Ngàm* was in *Bo Finyah's* compound. It was a compound he knew so well. He marched straight to the shrine where he was sitting and attending to people who had come to seek his help in fighting away evil spirits and sicknesses. As soon as *Bo Finyah* saw his old time friend, he smiled and whistled to the gods thanking them for what was about to happen. "A man who is trampled to death by an elephant is a man who is blind and deaf," he thought.

When it was Nyindô Ngàm's turn to be attended to, he walked in, greeted his old-time friend and placed the fowl and five cola nuts on a floor mat. The fowl crackled so loudly that it caused the seer to exhibit a broad smile which he rarely did. After the long smile he said:

"A man who bathes willingly with cold water shouldn't feel cold." Nyindô Ngàm looked at him but couldn't think of what to say. He stayed quiet until the seer spoke again.

"Here he is. Your son is alive as I prophesied. He lives with the burden of having been buried alive. How could you have buried your own son before his death, Nyindô Ngàm? Isn't old age supposed to bring us calm and wisdom? Why did you hurry? I don't say things I haven't seen. I say only what I see and I see what people don't see. When I say the things that are clear to me, people doubt me and I keep saying that those who only have mortal eyes shouldn't doubt what I see through the eye of the needle. This is him. He is alive and shall bury you as I said seven years ago. But you must first of all exhume him from where you buried him years ago due to your myopic refusal to listen to my advice," *Bo Finyah* concluded pointing to the fowl Nyindô Ngàm had brought.

"Bo Finyah, you deceived me. What did I do to you? Why did you allow me to send my son into the waiting hands of death?" Nyindô Ngàm asked. When he had left his house for Bo Finyah's shrine, he had expected him to at least apologise for having misled him in the past. Here he was asking questions that made him anxious and guilty.

"Did I miss out anything? Could there've been a mixed up somewhere?" he thought to himself.

"My blind friend, I thought age was supposed to make you wiser. Only a foolish man will have a dog and still bark instead of letting the dog do the barking. How can you have a seer-friend and still strain yourself trying to see for yourself instead of letting me do so? Why should a porcupine mourn the dead of a snake?" the seer asked staring at his client-friend.

This only confused Bo Bam the more. Did the renowned seer even understand what pain he was feeling in his left breast? He thought of taking his fowl and leaving the shrine without saying an additional word, but his age checked him and he had to exercise some patience and let the seer direct things. They sat quiet for some time but the seer kept looking into a black pot that stood before him as if he was reading a message from the gods through it. After a while, he picked up one of the cola nuts Bo Bam had brought, broke it and counted the lobes. They were seven. He smiled for the umpteenth time that morning and declared: "You move with the answers you seek look..." he went on, pointing again to the cock and showing the seven lobes of cola nut.

"See him. See the ignorant, innocent boy...look at Bam suffering and crying in pain because you buried him alive. These are the seven years he has been away suffering because of your hasty decisions. You refused to ask questions. Here he is after having gone through a lot, he returns to his roots where the birds, the wind and the streams will be friendly to him. Where he will find his true self again, where people will speak and he will understand what they say, where he can identify with, and recognise once more, the decency with which human beings are raised. He has lived in a world that knows no decency; a world where morality has been murdered and barbarism made the order of the day. Go home and welcome your son for he is of the gods and couldn't have been killed. Go and ask no questions for even the answers I give won't satisfy you. Only know that you never trusted me and went ahead to bury a stranger in the land of your fathers. Go home and prepare for the son of the soil is on his way. When he comes, bring him here let me wash away the things that block his way, let me wash away the ground you covered him with. It is only when I have exhumed him that he can start living again".

Bo Bam was filled with guilt yet couldn't understand why he had to be guilty. He couldn't see where he had gone wrong in burying his son who had been killed by a heavy load vehicle. He wondered if the right thing for him to have done then would've been to keep his son's corpse to decompose hoping that he was going to resurrect. That was how the so called Apostle Abel, one of the Pentecostal Christians in *Jerusalem Ministries of Fire Prayer*, a local church in Huba, kept his late mother's corpse for seven days following the advice of his pastor who said she was going to resurrect after three days like Jesus Christ did. After three days nothing happened yet he kept praying and fasting. On the seventh day, the entire neighbourhood smelt so badly but no one suspected that the smell was emanating from Abel's compound. It was first noticed by the village drunk, Ninying Pastis, who had gone to Abel's compound, as he was fond of doing, to steal sugarcane when he discovered that the farm was covered by a swamp of flies such that the sugarcane leaves could not even be seen at all. He ran back to the village and announced that what smelt in the village was in Abel's house. Initially, many people didn't take him seriously but when he insisted a couple of boys were sent to go and verify.

It was this story that kept Bo Bam's mind occupied for the

10

two minutes he sat quiet in *Bo Finyha's* shrine after his last words. The seer too was quiet and seemed to have made up his mind not to utter any other word. When Bo Bam tried to make further inquiries, Bo Finyah ignored him forcing him to return home in confusion and despair. While he was at the threshold, the seer said:

"If the arrow has not entered deeply then its removal is not hard." Bo Bam heard, but did not say anything because he had nothing to say.

***

Chapter Two

By the time *Nyindô Ngàm* reached his compound, breakfast had been prepared. It was his youngest wife's turn to feed him that week. Any other wife who had cooked anything special that day and wanted the lord of the compound to eat could bring it to his house. But it couldn't be the case with the food of the groin. Each wife in his compound had her week to feed him and grace his bed, and there could only be a change if he wanted to have something different or if the woman whose turn it was to grace his bed was suffering from the women's monthly sickness. That morning, *Na Yafi Nasah*, *Nyindô Ngàm*'s youngest wife, had cooked corn fufu and huckleberry.

It was the custom of the people of Huba to give or serve their guests and relatives with an odd number of anything that could be counted. Generally, a person would hand either one, three, five, seven or nine of anything he wanted them to have. Wives served their husbands with three, five or seven loaves of corn fufu depending on whether the husband was with a visitor or expecting one. In fact, visitors were always considered when serving food. The people lived together; they would celebrate or mourn with anybody whom either sorrow or fortune had visited. They worked and prayed for the same things; good health, good harvests, respectful wives and many children to bury them when they die. Visiting and receiving visitors was a normal thing to them. And when visitors came it was expected that food be given to them. It was considered a bad sign for a person not to have food for a visitor at any time of the day or for a visitor to refuse eating in a person's house.

If there was anything the Hubans lacked, it couldn't be food. Their soil was very fertile for the cultivation of assorted food crops. The large family sizes provided the adequate labour force required in the farm and guaranteed the availability of food in almost every home. In every home one visited, one could see large quantities of

12

corn, beans, yams, coco yams and plantains. Most compounds had extensive yards where some portions were used for the cultivation of vegitables such as: tomatoes, pepper, huckleberries and garden eggs.

His fourth wife knocked at the door and came in with a basket of corn fufu and huckleberry prepared with *egusi*. It was their cultural meal and Nyindô Ngàm particularly loved it so much. His huckleberry was never prepared with salt and maggi because he loved it natural.

"Lord, here is your food" she said placing the load on a dwarf table that stood behind the door.

Nyindô Ngàm cleared his throat, smiled and opened the basket. His smile broadened when he saw that it was corn fufu and that it had been wrapped in banana leaves. That was how he liked it, not tied in plastic papers. He remembered how in one of his wives' first days in his compound she went against her senior *mbanyas'* advice and wrapped corn fufu in plastic papers and he refused eating it.

His wife, with a plate in hand, was still standing in front of him enjoying the interest her husband was showing on the food she had prepared. She secretly hoped that later that evening he should have the same interest on the food she would present in the bedroom because her womanhood was crying for solace. When *Nyindô Ngàm* raised his head to look at her again he noticed that she looked more beautiful.

"*Na Bam* chose the land's most beautiful woman for me" he said to himself. The woman standing in front of him had been chosen and recommended to him by his first and most trusted wife, *Na Bam*, who always wanted the best for the family. He thought of how disturbing the last night had been and what it had cost him. He had been so disturbed about the storm that he hadn't had time to enter his wife's Jerusalem. Here he was preparing to eat corn fufu and *egusi* prepared by his wife but he just remembered that the previous

13

night he had failed to eat the *egusi* prepared in his wife by the gods.

"May tonight be better", he said to himself.

Na Yafi Nasah had been standing there for too long, longer than she'd wished. She coughed just to indicate that she was still there. He looked at her again and remembered that he was forgetting something. It was the plate the woman was holding that reminded him of what was escaping his memory.

"Bring that pot" he said, pointing to a pot that stood innocently by the hearth. When she brought it, he opened it and removing three pieces of meat from it said: "That is yours".

She bowed and left the house thanking her lord for what she considered a kind responsibility. When she had gone out, the father of the compound reflected a bit about the last night's happenings and the encounter he had had with *Bo Finyah* that morning. Many unanswered questions came to his mind; had he gone wrong in anything? What had been the reason for *Bo Finyah* to have spoken to him the way he did? What was he missing out? How could the son he buried years back be on his way as *Bo Finyah* mentioned? Where was the mix-up? Those were the questions that floated in his mind before another idea suddenly stroke him.

"Let me see," he said and got up from his seat and walked to one corner of the house where a brown handbag hung on the wall. It was the handbag his late son had left the house with the day he died. Those who were present at the scene of the accident reported that he died holding on to the small brown handbag. For the umpteenth time he opened the handbag and saw the same articles in it that he had seen both on the first day it was brought and the other days he opened it. The articles were: his late son's national identity card, a pen, a wrist watch which he could not remember ever seeing with his son and a packet of cigarette. Again, like in the other times he opened the handbag before he could recognise and identify his son with the items found in the bag except the wrist watch and the packet of cigarette. He had never known his son smoked. The police brought the bag saying he had been holding it in one hand and the

14

packet of cigarette in the other at the time of his death. He was unable to see the link between his late son and this packet of poison. It had been through the national identity card that the authorities managed to trace his family since his face was badly damaged beyond recognition in the accident.

After examining the bag and the contents again, the heavy hearted *Nyindô Ngàm* kept it back where he had taken it and settled down to have his meal. His mind was still so clouded but he was determined to eat before having a further thought on his predicaments.

He first went to the centre of the floor where a calabash of raffia wine stood and helped himself with his bull horn cup. When he filled it the first time, he gulped it down on the spot and filled it for the second time. This time around, he didn't drink; he took the content to where his chair was and after sitting he remembered he had forgotten something. Then he poured some of the wine from his cup on the floor murmuring something. For a very brief period after doing so his face seemed to brighten up a bit but the expression suddenly changed and once more his face became dull and frightening. He spent the first few moments in sipping the contents of the cup after which he kept it on a stool by his right and settled down to eat. A bowl of water was standing by the food his wife had brought. Sitting on his cane chair Nyindô Ngàm carefully washed his hands.

The children had already had their breakfast and were playing in the yard while Nyindô Ngàm's third wife, Bih Njua, was spreading her laundry on the broad dwarf cypress that stood at the centre of the compound when suddenly one of the kids indicated that a strange looking man was lazily walking into the compound. The woman raised her head to see who it was.

"Do we have a visitor?" she thought to herself unable to recognise who the man dressed in a black t-shirt, a blue pair of jeans trousers, a pair of old brown sandals and a red fez cap, was. When she stepped forward and took a closer look at the man, she felt strange. Her hair

15

stood on ends, her armpits itched and she felt goose pimples all over her body.

"There is something cynical about this man" she concluded and decided to greet the stranger and find out whether he had missed his way. Before the stranger could respond she recognised where she was and who she was standing with. She was in her husband's compound and standing face to face with Bam's ghost. She couldn't hold herself any longer.

"Booooooo! I am finished. Ghosssssssst" she shouted and removing her slippers, ran pass the door to her house and went to the backyard without being conscious of where she was going to. The whole compound reverberated with the sound of her voice moments after she had stopped. Every other woman and their children came out to see what was happening to their co-wife and mother. Those who had known Bam before his sudden death seven years back were seized by panic and immediately took to their heels as soon as they saw who was standing in the centre of the compound. Within them they were all certain that they had seen a ghost in broad day light. The commotion was terrible as women could be seen bumping one another and some even stepping on children without minding to stop or look back. They were sure that Bam's ghost had come to haunt them and each and everyone of them was running for their dear life.

Nyindô Ngàm had just finished washing his hands and was yet to begin eating when he heard people shouting in his yard. Satisfying the hunger of his stomach became secondary. He was anxious to find out what had caused the uproar. He immediately knew that something strange was happening in his compound that morning but he could not figure out what exactly it was.

"Maybe the pregnant night has given birth to a headless baby" he tried to figure out hoping nothing too bad was happening.

By the time he stepped out of his house; the women, children and a few neighbours were hiding and peeping from behind different houses and trees. The figure that was causing the panic stood at the centre of the compound looking frightened itself. *Nyindô Ngàm* could clearly recognise that that was the image of his son. Though seven years had gone by, he could still recognise his son standing at the centre of the compound not able to understand why everybody was running away from him. On seeing his father, he made an attempt to move towards him but was stopped by his father's hand gesture. His father stood there, as a man would after overcoming his initial fear. In just a second a series of thoughts ran through his mind. Even if he had to run where would he run to?

"Does a man not run from trouble outside to his compound? How then can I run away from my compound? Whatever it is I will face it" he said to himself.

"Baba!" the figure spoke for the first time. From his voice, one could discern the failure, frustration, shame and the pain he was bringing home from Ednouaya or, as far as the people were concerned, from his grave, after seven long years.

His father thought he recognised the voice. It had not changed much except that it was now heavy with sorrow and pain unduly suffered. It was his son. Then the words of the seer began to make some sense to him. He gathered courage and called his son's name.

"Bam! Is this you or it is your ghost?"

"Yes father, it is me. Why is everybody running away from me? Did you people hear that I was dead?" he asked.

"Mm m m my son! Mm m my all! You won't understand. We buried you. You were buried alive" he said feeling guilty. His voice was heavy and did not sound well even to his ears. Look there, that is your grave" he went on pointing to a corner where they had buried the accident victim that was brought and presented to them seven years ago as Bam.

"I am still alive, father. How can everyone run away from me, your son?" Bam said. After looking at each other for some time Bo Bam heaved a dry sigh, looked up to the sky before he spoke to his son again.

"Come in let me show you something," he invited him while taking

17

the lead for them to move away from where they had been standing for some minutes.

He noticed that his steps were not steady and his eyes were weak. However, he moved back into his house while Bam followed him. At this time, many more people after hearing the shouts were flowing into the compound. Those who had run completely out of the compound were beginning to return from their hideouts hoping to see how possible it was that their husband, father and neighbour was chatting with a spirit, a ghost. When father and son moved into the house, the crowd stood at the door straining their necks to get hints of the discussion between father and the ghost from within.

Nyindô Ngàm's three neighbours – Timchia, Kuma and Mbah moved into the house to help him confront the reality. They too agreed that who they were seeing was Bam who had left the village seven years back for the State University of Ednuoaya 1 in the French speaking section of the bilingual Republic of Nooremaca and had been reported dead that same day. They could also recall that when his mutilated corpse was brought to the village the day after the accident, it was buried in their presence and in this very compound.

Once in the house, the three men fetched seats for themselves. Their legs were already too weak to carry them for long after what they had seen and were about to hear. Bam stood there unable to understand himself and everyone around him. He had escaped from the hardship of Ednuoaya with the aim of returning home to have some rest, meet his family and receive a new dose of blessings from his father but his home, as it stood now, had something different for him. *Nyindô Ngàm* quietly and lackadaisically moved to where the symbolic brown handbag had always hung for seven years now. He took it, brought it and placed at the centre of the house, then went to his seat.

"This is my bag" Bam burst out after seeing the bag he had lost on his way to Ednuoaya seven long years ago.

"Yes, we thought so too, that is why we believed it was you a car had killed that fateful day when this bag was brought to us along with a mutilated corpse. Tell us, what happened? Where have you been all these years? Who did we burry in your name?

"If he has come *Nyindô Ngàm* and you believe as I do believe now that he is really your son and not a ghost or an evil spirit that has taken your son's form, wouldn't it be wise for him to eat something before speaking to us?" said Timchia licking his lips after seeing the basket of corn fufu on the floor. It was like Timchia, he never joked with food. It was said of him in the village that he could eat five loaves of corn fufu with only one raw garden egg. *"Never throw away or play with food"* was his policy and the doctrine he always taught his children. It was rumoured that he once got his first son severely beaten for refusing to eat in someone's house. Everyone present knew that what he just said about Bam eating first was not said out of concern for him or the family but simply because he speculated that if Bam were to eat it would've been but normal for everyone including him to eat. His tactics failed him this time because everyone ignored him. They were all anxious to hear the story Bam was about to narrate about his "death and possible resurrection".

Bam sat down, removed his cap and narrated the story of his life to the men from the day he left Huba for Ednuoaya. When he started speaking, his mother ran into the house wailing but the men shouted her down and ordered her to leave the house if she couldn't stay quiet. She managed to gulp down the rest of her wailing but was unable to push back her river of tears. She sat on the floor sobbing as her son spoke.

***

Chapter Three

I decided to come back home to my family because our people say that if a man is in harmony with his family, that is success. I couldn't remain the lone stick out there for I would have been destroyed. I came home to see you and reunite with my own since our people believe that sticks in a bundle are unbreakable.

The story of my struggle is a long one. So long that I do not know from which end I have to begin. And I hate telling stories. Yet I have to tell you this one for you to know what I have gone through and what our brothers go through in the hands of our other *brothers* in the other part of this country. We have suffered for many generations but have refused to dissolve as they thought we would. I have to tell my story for those who know anything already know that as long as the leopard has no historians it is the exploits of the hunter that will be celebrated rather than the bravery of the leopard.

Where do I begin? Let me see, okay I will begin from the day I was preparing to leave this sacred land of my ancestors to the strange terrifying French speaking part of this mutilated country where I suffered discrimination, suppression and subjugation in every area of my life from a people who, by all standards, are not better than we are. It is true that where water is the boss there the land must obey. I returned so empty, tired and consumed by the vultures of this country. I assure you that Nooremaca is not a place. President Aybia Lapua and his evil collaborators have destroyed this country. Those who are at the top have refused to give others a chance. They keep recycling their lives and punishing innocent ones. And it seems **even death has sided with the corrupt officials of the government** of the Republic of Nooremaca. Old age has come but death has refused to take them away from the surface of this earth in order to rescue us from their torture. They say they are retired but not tired and we keep hearing the same names that were heard by those who were born before us. This country has no future because it is ruled by evil men who have no vision for the youths.

I now understand what the Kenyan lawyer and professor, Patrick Loch Otieno Lumumba means when he says that: "The problem with Africa is that those who have power have no ideas and those who have ideas have no power". His idea holds very true to the situation in this country because we have allowed power in the hands of those who have no wisdom on how to use the power and who rather use it to abuse our freedom. The only way to succeed in this country, it seems, is to join them because there is no space for good people here. Martyrs fill the prison cells while evil men parade the streets and are rewarded for their cruelty. I am a victim and a survivor of their evil acts. What should I even say? Let me start from the beginning as I have promised. I hope I remember the things that matter.

Father, this story I am about to recount is the only thing I have achieved in my seven years of being out of this land. It is the only thing I have returned with that I hope to share with you. In fact, permit me tell not only you, but the entire world so that I can even say the things you already know.

The day before I left for Ednuoaya, where I had to enrol in the prestigious university of Ednuoaya 1, my father took me to *Bo Finyah*'s shrine to find out from him if he could read any message from the gods about my life and the journey I was undertaking. I still remember some of the things he said that day.

'Thank the gods you brought this boy to this shrine,' the seer had said.

'The other side of this country is full of evil people but the enemy carrying your son's photo is from this side of the country and I see you burying your son alive,' he had said. He was quiet for some time before talking again.

'You must ask questions when the time comes because I see your son standing on one side of the road and his helper on the other side.

21

They are both looking for each other but you are blocking them from meeting. They will push him down in order to climb up. This world is a jungle but I assure you that Bam shall go and return alive. He shall face many manmade obstacles on his way, people will lie about him to a red dog and throw stones to block him…,' the seer told my father. He was quiet again for some time after which he looked at me and smiled before speaking again.

'…but my son, step on the stones and move forward. Also remember that the skin of the leopard is beautiful, but not his heart. Be patient and you will come to understand that patience can cook a stone. Refuse to die for you are destined to live till you bury your father when he shall leave from here. But you must remain true to yourself and to others. Fight against evil and speak the truth at all times. And don't forget that those people treat us as if we are foreigners. You are a destined child, but remember that even the lion that is the king of the forest protects himself against flies. Rats don't dance in the cat's doorway. My son, eat only what you have earned and what has been given to you and never eat what has been stolen' he told me before turning again to my father.

'If he does as I have said, life will be fair to him. There is nothing on earth that is bigger than being alive. Only life is above life', he said and turning to me again continued.

'Son, you will die only when your death comes. The sea is rough, but should boats stop sailing? I see a man of your height and size but without a face holding your picture and running away from you into his death. Nyindô Ngàm, only you have to be patient and ask questions when that day comes. Do not see a stranger with your son's shoes and conclude that he is your son' he ended.

Those were the things he said and after washing me with ìlôl he blessed me and asked us to leave. After we returned home that day, my father called me into this house and spoke to me about my future. He told me that he wanted to teach me one lesson in life and that I have to take it seriously. I sat quiet and waited for him to speak. This was exactly where I sat that day. He said to me.

22

'My son, you are the light that should shine in this land even after I have left. You are going to a land I have never gone to because I never had the chance to and because education was not so important in our time. I am letting you go because of the breed you are made of and I am very sure you'll succeed. Always remember where you come from. Never forget your family because a family, they say, is like a forest, when you are outside it is dense, when you are inside you see that each tree has its place. There is one thing, my son, which you must not allow to derail you in life. That thing is a woman. A woman is the devil herself, a snake and you must always put dry leaves around you whenever you are around women so that if they make any move you will get from the sound of the leaves and know their direction so as to avoid them. I want to make you understand that I mean all women; your mother and all the women in this compound included. Even my late mother, she was a devil. Can you remember how my mother was before she died?' my father asked.

'Yes, I can. She was blind and could not walk on her own. I always carried her to the latrine' I responded.

'What would she do after you've taken her to the latrine and back?' my father asked again.

'She would cuss and insult me' I said.

'Good! That means you can still remember' he went on. 'That is how all women are. They are never grateful and you should never live life to please a woman because it is practically impossible to do so. Even God could not please them. They've shown that they are not happy the way God created them. Our women here are even better. In Ednuoaya where you are going to you'll see girls and women who've demonstrated outright dislike to the way God created them, women who shave their eyebrows and draw them with pencil, have rings on their noses, and even pay men to sleep with them so that they take away their luck. You have to recognise them and flee before they destroy your life. In fact, flee from all women' he concluded.

I didn't really understand what my father meant by that but I didn't bother to ask any questions. I thought he was wrong in saying that my mother was a devil. Maybe his mother was but not my mother. I didn't think my mother was wicked in any way. She was the best woman I'd ever seen and when I was still a kid, I always thought that were she not married to my father, I would've married her.

Later that day, I thought of the discussion I had with my father and started considering his opinion about women. I remembered a poem I had read titled *My Woman is Tiger* by Bole Butake. In the poem the persona celebrates the physical beauty of his woman but condemns her treatment of the man and her fierce tiger-like behaviour towards him. If a university professor like Bole Butake could write this about a woman, then my father might not have been wrong in his hypothesis. After a period of serious reflection, I concluded that it couldn't be all women. The problem with my father's argument was that he considered all women to be evil. Yet he got married to many of them. What did he expect of me?

***

My mother was the only one who was sceptical about my father's plans for me to travel to Ednuoaya. I can remember the attempts she made to discourage my father the day he raised the idea suggested by my high school teacher who said it was wrong for a bright student like me to stay in the village after having passed the G.C.E Advanced level in four subjects. My mother said there was no need acquiring further education. She said my father was sending me away for witches and wizards to kill. She even stated examples of some people she knew who had travelled to Ednuoaya to school in the universities of Ednuoaya 1 and Ednuoaya 2 but always ended up as palm wine tappers in the village because book in those schools was taught in a language they did not understand.

'Those people encouraging him to abandon me here and go in search of knowledge are all living in this village and taking care of their ailing parents. Why don't they go themselves? Is Bam not teaching in the village college here and earning some money for himself? Let him stay here, get a wife and start his own family. Don't you know that those book heads do not end up marrying?' she complained.

My father ignored her ranting and went ahead with preparations for me to travel to Ednuoaya in October that year. But I felt guilty after listening to my mother's worries. My dream was to become a university lecturer one day and travelling to Ednuoaya was an opportunity for me to realise that dream. I decided that going there was the only way for me to ever qualify to bear the title of a professor. Just imagine people addressing me as Professor Bam. That sounds good, doesn't it? My mother was trying to stand between me and my dream with her lamentations and nagging about the subject of my going to the university. Her complaints made me feel guilty because I had recently read Fale Wache's "Lament of a Mother". I only consoled myself that I was not going to behave like Ndikochong who had abandoned his mother for thirty years under the pretext that he was going to school.

The following day, my mother raised the issue again pointing out to my father that Ednuoaya was too far from home and that I didn't know how to speak French which was the language used in that part of the country. She suggested to my father that if his mind was already made up on sending me to the university, then he could as well send me to the then newly created state university of Adnemada. It was the second state university in that English part of the country in over fifty years of the country's independence from colonial rule. My father saw that idea as an option and sent for Mr L.C.M, the teacher who had initially suggested to him that I should go to the university, to discuss it with him before taking a final decision. The teacher's full name was Leng Chah Manuel but he always abbreviated it as L.C.M. After discussing with him, Mr, L.C.M revealed that it was impossible. I was present when my father asked him whether it was possible for me to study in the newly created university of Adnemada.

'If that had been possible I would have first suggested it to you,

25

father'. He told my father and went ahead to explain that the institution had just been newly created for political pacification and that only the faculty of science was functional at that time. He added that he had heard from a reliable source that over eighty-five percent of the lecturers there were Froncophones from Ednuoaya, Alauodaa and other francophone universities in the country who knew nothing in English. Since I was arts inclined, that option of me going to the University of Adnemada was completely wiped out from the plan and I had to travel to that far away land. He said he would have preferred the University of Aeaba which was purely Anglo-Saxon, but didn't do so because my father had earlier indicated that he only had someone in Ednuoaya with whom I could live and study. He didn't want me to go to a place where he knew no one he could trust. It sounded strange to me but my desire to succeed and become a great man in future made me ignore the strange feeling and all I could imagine was a beautiful future of me sitting in an office in a university abroad or even in this country reading through books and writing some.

After the meeting with Mr L.C.M, my father filled his cup with raffia wine, drank a bit and gave me to drink from the same cup. That was the third time I was having the honour of drinking from my father's cup. The first time was when I started clearing my mothers' farms for the season's planting. On the first day of clearing, my mother came to the farm and after seeing the portion I had cleared was very happy with me that she returned home and reported to my father, praising me for the good work. Later that evening, my father called me to his house and congratulated me and gave me some palm wine from his cup. Something he rarely did. I felt so happy, recognised and important to my family that the following day I did even better. My mother saw that I had done even better, but it didn't surprise her for she knew that when a labourer is praised his cutlass begins to cut more keenly. The second time I drank from that cup was after I passed the Nooremaca General Certificate of Education Examination ordinary level. He called me into his hut and declared to me that I was the first in their entire family to have brought him that honour. However, he told me to

26

always remember that it was not going to be easy because the lead cow gets whipped the most. After listening to him and drinking from his cup of mystery, my determination to work harder and pass in the N.G.C.E Examination increased. For many months I kept hearing my father's voice prophesy to me.

"My son, the previous generations in this family have always eaten what the soil can offer them. I tell you that all monkeys cannot hang on the same branch because times have changed. The red man's machines have destroyed our forests and our soils, and farming is no longer what the future generation should hope on. Let that dream of mine begin with you. No person is born great, my son; great people become great when others are sleeping. I know it is difficult beginning alone but remember that the strong do not need clubs; you can do it alone. When you succeed, drag others along because a single bracelet does not jingle."

Most of my meetings with my father usually ended in the same way. He would ask me if I had understood all he had been telling me. I always answered in the affirmative even though sometimes I found it difficult to make sense from some of his proverbs. Whenever I said I had understood, he would say one more thing before dismissing me. He would always end with this statement:

"My son, I speak to you in proverbs because a proverb is the horse that can carry one swiftly to the discovery of ideas. You can leave."

That was the third time I was drinking from his cup, it seems he wasn't in the mood for proverbs. He only wanted me to receive that dose of blessing and when I did, he asked me to go and inform my mothers and siblings that I was travelling to Ednuoaya in October that year. It was in August that we had that discussion. Everybody was extremely happy when I told them I was leaving the village to one day return as a better person, but my mother was very worried. The fear of her losing me was more than the joy of ever seeing me a better person in future. To her, the ambition was not necessary. She knew that a man's life ended in him being born, growing up to become a full man, building a compound, marrying

27

as many wives as he could handle and making many children who would help in cultivating the expansive acres of land that the village had. However, she still reluctantly went ahead to bless me knowing she couldn't have done anything contrary when the lord of her life was in support of my travelling to Ednuoaya where I was expected to pursue university studies. My mother saw that she couldn't win in this battle and had to give up. She never spoke about it to my hearing until the day of my departure.

***

If relatives are united and help each other, what evil can hurt them? In the morning of the day I was supposed to travel, my father called me into this house and performed some cultural rites. He asked me to kneel down and put my hands together as if I was forming a little bowl. I did as he had ordered. He poured raffia wine into my cupped hands and asked me to drink. He did it three times after which he asked me to wash my hands with some of it. When he was through, he sent me to my mother's hut to receive her own dose of blessings. At the time I got there all my father's wives were present. They were seated on the two beds that were in my mother's hut as if they were mourning. There was a small stool at the centre of the house for me to sit on. I understood and sat on it without anyone telling me to. The person who would have told me was my mother but she looked so weak from having to miss me. After sitting for a few moments, I saw my mother move for the first time since I entered. She came to where I was sitting and holding a calabash of some slimy liquid she bent over me to perform the rite. I knew what it was. It was water mixed with ilôl, a strong sacred herbal substance used in washing people in my village. It was the same substance that Bo Finyah had washed me with earlier in his shrine. She carried some of the liquid with her left hand three times and gave me to drink after which she used some in washing my face and feet. My other mothers watched her perform the rite and in the end they all wished me good luck. When the exercise was done, I felt

28

so spiritually fortified and uplifted that I thought I could overcome every obstacle that came my way.

Later on that morning, many of our neighbours and well-wishers brought some food items for me to take along. It was proof that it takes a whole village to raise a child. The news that I was travelling had spread round the village like the scent of burnt pepper. Everybody knew, and brought bunches of plantains, beans, corn, *garri*, dried meat and vegetables for me to travel with. I couldn't have taken all the gifts so they had to be kept in my mother's house. She insisted that I take some but I refused because I didn't even know where I was going and thought it would be tedious carrying a heavy load. When she saw that I was serious about my decision of not carrying any load, she gave up on persuading me. I was happy and went on with my preparation which was largely psychological rather than physical. I needed to be sure I had completely made up my mind to travel and that I was at peace with myself and my roots.

At exactly 11:00am that day I was on my way to the Gnodnufa motor park where I had to board a bus for Adnemada town. Among those who had come to see me off at the motor park were my mother, one of her *mbanyas* and eight of my siblings. I had no luggage except my brown handbag and another small bag containing my few clothes and documents which one of my younger brothers carried. They were all excited that I was travelling to town, the place that had the powers to make me greater than every other person in the village except the *Foyn*. On our way to the park they chatted with every age mate of theirs who cared to listen to them brag that their *big brother* was travelling to the country's political capital where His Almighty Reverend Excellency, the President of the United Republic of Nooremaca lived. They even lied that the president had written a letter inviting me to come and give him advice on how he could better rule this country. The kids knew that my siblings were joking about me being the president's adviser. However, they believed that I was going to the national capital to return one day as a big man with a potbelly and in one of those big cars they only saw in Pa Ubia's television.

Pa Ubia was an old businessman who had spent half of his life in the state of Ubia in Airegina, a neighbouring country to Nooremaca. He had only returned to settle here in his native land with his wives and children ten years before the year I was leaving the village. He was the only rich man who had a generator and a television set in the neighbourhood at that time. When I was still a little boy, my friends and I would go and fetch water and firewood for that compound just to be permitted to watch the television. After doing that, we would wash our bodies so well in order to be clean enough to be permitted to sit on the floor and watch the television. There were days we went there and there was no TV signal but we would stay there the whole time watching a TV that showed no images, only *"rice"* as we used to describe it. And whenever we returned to our homes we would feel so happy for having wasted our lives there in the name of watching TV. It was only as I grew older that I realised what a waste of time it had been. If only I had used that time to explore books!

While at the motor park, I saw sadness in my mother's eyes. She wasn't happy about me leaving them and going to a strange land. She was trying so hard to hold back the tears that were threatening to flow as she spoke to me for the last time. When she opened her mouth to speak, her voice did not sound like the voice I knew. It was broken and her expressions didn't come out naturally.

'My son … if only … a wo…man could make … a decision … that … would … be res… respected' she struggled to say but it didn't sound the way she'd wanted it to. She stayed quiet for some time and composed herself before speaking again. When she spoke this time her words came more fluently but fast as though she was hurrying to leave in order not to betray herself.

'Go well and in whatever thing you do remember that your umbilical cord was buried in this land. Never forget that there is a power above you called God. Pray to him when in difficulties. I have always done well to people hoping that my children will benefit from that. I believe that because of the good things I have done to others, God in

His goodness will direct people of good will to you. Come, my son' she said stretching out her hands to embrace me. Her embrace was warm and I felt like staying in her arms. What I experienced was pure love and unreserved affection.

"My son, I wish you stayed and got married first, our people say a single stick may smoke, but it will not burn. You will be alone in that world, but do not accept to be broken. Struggle and always be stronger than your oppressor. Something dropped on my shoulder like a drop of rain and I later realised it was a drop of her tears. She cried and when she released me from her arms she didn't speak again. She also tried her best to prevent me from seeing her face. I felt so sad and tears started running down my cheeks too. She noticed it and left without saying a word. It was one of my stepmothers who spoke to me. Her talk was brief because her heart was heavy too.

'We cry now that you're leaving us. Our son, make us smile tomorrow when you return. Make us know that it was a risk worth taking. Safe journey our son' she ended.

After my two mothers were gone, my siblings lingered at the motor park until the bus finally took off forty-five minutes later. I gave 100france to each of them and they all bade me farewell and ran homeward.

As soon as the bus took off, a certain measure of confidence arrested me. I felt as ambitious as Ngwe Nkemasaah in John Nkemngong Nkengasong's *Across the Mongolo* when he was leaving Atah to Besaadi where he hoped to study hard so as to one day become the president of his country. When I thought of Nkengasong's character, Ngwe, I became afraid because I could see many similarities between my life and the character's. At this stage, I became afraid that I could in the end fail to succeed and end up like Ngwe who set his ambitions too high and ended up getting mad without achieving any. However, I consoled myself by concluding that there was a huge difference between Nkengasong's character and myself. One, I established that Ngwe had set out to become the president of his country whereas I only wanted to become a

31

university lecturer. There could only be one president in a country. That is probably why Ngwe did not succeed unlike the case with being a lecturer because the country could have many lecturers at a time. Secondly, I remembered that some natives in Ngwe's village such as Mbe Benu might not have been happy about him achieving anything. My case was different because my land was made up of kind hearted people who wanted to help each other achieve their dreams.

My mind took me to another book I had read. It was Francis Ateh's *Between Two Worlds* whose main character, Ndong, had run away from the village to the red man's land without his fathers' blessings. Yet he ended up succeeding. It was going to be even easier for me to succeed because I had my determination, my parents' blessings and God's guidance to count on. I knew I was a hunter who was sure to return home with game that would make every waiter happy. I was very sure of my purpose and took a resolution to stay focused until I attained the apex of greatness which to me was to become a lecturer of African literatures and civilisations in top universities in Africa and beyond.

When I reached Adnemada town, it was already 4:00pm and the main thing I had to do was to buy a bus ticket for the nation's political capital. I didn't face difficulties locating the travel agency because I had told the driver who carried me from Huba that I didn't know the Bus Station. So when we reached the Mile 3 Junction, he showed me the park of one of the agencies that was travelling to Ednuoaya. The name of the agency was SAFE JOURNEYS VOYAGES.

Many people were travelling that night and it was relatively tedious for one to pay for the travel ticket. I saw people standing in queues and when I asked to know why, I was told that they were paying their bus tickets to travel to different towns of the republic of Nooremaca. Some were travelling to Ebmila, others to Alauoda and other cities. I was shown where to pay a ticket for Ednuoaya. I went to the line for the passengers travelling to the same destination with me and joined the queue. It took me about seven minutes to reach the counter. I was told by the woman at the counter that a ticket to Nooremaca was 5,600france. I searched in my pockets and pulled out the money my father had given me. It was 88,500france. The money was to serve as transportation to Ednuoaya, tuition for the 2013/2014 academic year and other expenses. I had to be careful with the money and manage it as best as I could. After removing 6,000france and giving to the cashier, she requested to have my national identity card which I also took out and handed over to her. She copied out my name on the ticket and asked me which seat number I wanted to take. The question was embarrassing to me because I hadn't anticipated that before. However I told her my day of birth which is 11th and she scribbled 11 on the receipt. When she was done, she gave me my identity card, my change and the ticket. On the ticket she had circled the three things that were very important. They were the time of departure, the seat number and the bus number. That made it easy for me to trace the bus. After looking through the ticket I put everything in my brown handbag. When I turned to leave, I noticed that one dirty shabbily dressed guy was looking at me in a way that made me feel uncomfortable. He was certainly a thief calculating a victim. I assured myself that if that was the case then I was not going to be his victim.

I left the counter and moved to the open space where buses were parked to see if I could locate the bus with the number written on my ticket. It turned out to be difficult which frightened me as I checked all the seven buses but didn't see any with the number I had been given. It was only when I inquired from someone working at the agency that I was told my bus was at the washing point. I identified that he was working for the agency because he was wearing the agency's t-shirt. I decided to call the number my father had given me. The owner of the number was supposed to receive me in Ednuoaya the following morning and provide accommodation for me for a month or two while I get another place to live in. I say another place as if I had enough money to pay rents. In fact I knew he was to lodge me until when he decides to send me out of his house. I went to a call box and dialled the number and someone answered. I didn't want to speak first so I listened to know whether it was a man or a woman, and then came a masculine voice.

'Oui, c'est qui?' the person spoke. I got choked when I heard the person speak to me in a language I wasn't familiar with. In a short while, I pictured how difficult life would be in that francophone part of the country. My mother's expressed fears clouded my mind and for a moment I thought she had been right in trying to stop me from travelling. How was I to cope with French? I was still in Adnemada and someone who was supposed to be my host in Ednuoaya was already speaking French to me over the phone. He had been waiting for some seconds while these thoughts ran through my mind. I decided to speak in English. After all, English was the only colonial language I knew or rather the only colonial language I thought I knew.

'Hello, I … I am Bam Marcel Mubang, son of Ayong-nhi à Bobo Bam I mean Nyindô Ngàm of Huba. My father asked me to call you after paying my ticket' I said.

'Bam, a-n-ghi va' bä?' he asked in Huba. I felt a sigh of relieve knowing that he was from the same village as me. He went ahead to instruct me on how to behave from that time till the next morning when I was expected to reach Ednuoaya. He insisted that I call him as soon as I reach and ended by wishing me a safe journey and when he dropped the call I felt renewed strength and determination in me. I felt a reassuring sense of security.

Our bus had still not been brought to the park and judging from the time written on my ticket, it was still too early for me to start anticipating leaving soon. It was difficult to sit doing nothing – only waiting and constantly looking at the time. I sat on a bench at the bus station watching the lazy foot of time move as though it was against my journey. I tried to distract myself and make time move faster by watching a football match on TV between Liverpool and Chelsea. The television was attached to the door of a drinking spot at the bus station. Many people didn't even have time for the match because it was a replay. Only those like myself who had no other thing doing could stand there and watch. I thought of the days

34

we used to negotiate with Pa Ubia's children and even perform their tasks just to be allowed to watch their outdated television. Here I was standing in front of a bigger TV and no one was bothering to even watch.

After loitering at the bus station for what I estimated was four hours I looked at the time and it was still 5:30pm. The bus I was to travel in was not yet at the station. I felt bored and very tired. Going by the time written on my ticket I knew I still had to wait for about two hours thirty minutes. I say it as if people respect time in this country. 8:00pm to most time conscious people means 10:00pm here, even today. That is why we keep lagging behind.

The bus was eventually brought at 7:17pm. I went there to check if the door was open so I could sit in while waiting but noticed that all the doors were locked. I loitered there with some other travellers for a long time but there were no signs of anyone opening the bus for us. Some women became impatient and started ranting.

A girl walked towards our bus. Her beauty hit my chest as I stared at her in complete admiration, and thanking the gods for having brought me this far. She wore a black t-shirt over a pair of tight-fitting blue jeans trousers. Her beautiful black face was a great charm, but her graceful walk and tantalizing behind were more so. It was difficult to say which aspect of her was more noticeable. The charm in her walk was irresistible as she moved like a mother duck. Her elaborate hairstyle looked like it had been done with bags of mesh. I doubted whether she could see with her left eye as the mesh extended to her cheek completely covering that eye. I thought of what my father had said about women and smiled. To me, women were the most interesting creatures on earth.

It was at 8:50pm that the doors to the bus were opened. I stood there and watched how people scrambled into the bus and struggled to locate their seats. I was almost at the door when I felt an urge to make water. I took an about turn and went back to see if I could urinate. At the park I saw for the first time that there was an opened room with "RECEPTION" boldly written on the door. I knocked at the door and went in. There were a few people in there, probably other travellers, taking out their bags. The receptionist showed me where the toilet was. At the door to the toilet was a young man holding toilet paper. He was standing directly at the door; blocking it but I could see that there were people inside. I greeted him and tried squeezing myself in but he blocked me.

'*Na nwan hundre*' he said in his funny Pidgin. I handed to him 100france and he let me enter. While in there, I decided they were not going to just squander my money for nothing. I had to empty all the shit I had in my stomach – all the yam, cassava, maize and corn **fufu I had eaten that morning back in Huba.** After I had finished I decided to separate my money. I counted 85,000france and put in the pocket of the pair of shorts I had inside. The rest of the money was put in my back pocket and a few coins put in my handbag. With that I hoped to buy something to eat on the way.

By the time I returned our bus had been moved from its **initial position but I didn't face any difficulties locating it since it** wasn't taken very far away from its initial spot. Holding my ticket in my hand, I majestically moved to where the bus was now stationed with its engine steaming with lights on. People were still entering. You only had to hand your ticket to a man standing by the door whose job was to cut the ticket into two and give you the bigger piece. This was their form of control. I gave my ticket to the guy doing the checking. Instead of cutting it as it was done to others, he held it and turned to discuss with a man whom I later realised **was the bus driver. Two metres behind me was a figure that looked** familiar to me. It was already dark but I could recognise that it was the same guy whose eyes had followed me at the counter over four hours back. This time, not only were his eyes following me but his whole body. He even looked more suspicious to me then. I think it was only to me because other people were not moved. He didn't seem to be coming towards the bus, yet he wasn't going back either. He only stood there pretending to be manipulating his phone. The *motor boy* turned and gave my ticket and indicated that I should enter the bus. I was on the second step of the bus when something pulled me back. I turned just to notice a shadow disappearing into darkness behind the toilet. I shouted that someone had seized my bag. A couple of men ran towards the direction but the thief had flown already. Many people showed concerned and asked if I had money in it. I told them the most important thing in the bag was my national identity card. They were all disturbed and expressed doubts on whether I would reach Ednuoaya with the numerous checkpoints on the way. The driver said the thief was gone and proposed that I give him some money so that he could bribe the gendarmes on the way. That was the only solution if I still wanted to travel.

'How much should I give you, sir?' I asked him.

'*Fap bag*' he said. I immediately understood how much he meant. I was still trying to unzip my trousers to remove the money I had inside when a woman opted to help. She gave me 2,000france. Other good Samaritans chipped in what they had and at the end I had 9,750france in my hands. Everyone wanted to offer help to me – some with money and some with words of comfort.

'Isn't this what my mother meant when she said people will help me?' I said to myself wondering why my father had tried to make me hate women. It was a woman who started the kind hearted gesture. In the end I handed over all the money to the bus driver, who removed 5,000france and gave me back the rest of the money saying;

'*When you go reach Ednuoaya go use som da moni fix new adentiti dey. Dis contri no good*'.

I felt so grateful to the people in that bus for their assistance. After all I hadn't lost much money in the bag. The 4,750france I was now holding was enough to cover the money that was in that bag and even buy another bag. The only problem I had was how to make a new national identity card in a foreign land. After serious thoughts I convinced and reassured myself that the *Uncle* who was to pick me up at the park would certainly assist me establish a new one.

After that incident, I tried as much as I could to ignore the homesickness that was grabbing me by the throat but it was difficult. I kept thinking of the birds, the vast green lands, the animals and abundant food. I wondered if I could ever be a happy person living so far away from the land of my birth.

'Can fish survive out of water?' I asked aloud to myself before realising that people didn't need to hear my thoughts.

The journey from Adnemada to my final destination, Ednuoaya, was expected to last nine hours as I was told. The normal duration was six hours if the road was in good condition, but that was not the situation with the roads in the country. Especially in this side of the country which the government has completely removed from her development scheme because it is notorious for opposing the regime. Needless to say that the road was in a deplorable state as one could see several potholes from Adnemada to Ednuoaya. Those passengers who were already familiar with the deplorable state of the Adnemada – Ednuoaya road started complaining when we were still at the park. The roads in my village were better. Although most of them were not tarred, they at least were smooth. Community work was alive there and many of the villagers understood the bias of the francophone dominated administration and made up their minds to live without expecting government assistance. They constantly renewed and kept their roads in good condition by emptying gutters, repairing bridges and filling potholes. After thinking of the beautiful vegetation of my homeland and the industriousness of its people I had no choice but to support the claim Margaret Afuh expresses in her poem – *To Countryside* that nature is the 'pain-healing balm', and that a countryside is the 'generator of virtues diverse'.

Even though the Adnemada – Ednuoaya road was in a desperate state of dilapidation as a result of neglect, it was an advantage. I say so because accidents hardly occurred on that road compared to the relatively good roads in the country. Its deplorable state necessitated drivers to drive more cautiously. Roads linking major Francophone towns such as the Alauoda – Ednuoaya road were the altars where the blood of innocent citizens was constantly drunk. This was due to the relatively good condition of the roads which motivated drivers to over speed thereby leading to constant head-to-head collisions. I was lost in thought about my village and family when the *motor boy* gave three long hoots on the car horn.

'*Hooooooooooooooooot hooooooooooooooooooot hooooooooooooooooooot*' it sounded.

Those who had already been sleeping woke up and wiped their eyes. Those hoots were to prepare the passengers' minds that the bus was leaving not long from that time and to alert those who were not yet in the bus to hurry up.

Chapter Four

At 10:10pm the driver hooted again, indicating that we were leaving. Almost all the passengers bowed their heads to ask God for journey mercies. I remembered that I earlier observed a similar thing when we were leaving the Gnodnufa motor park back in the village. All passengers bowed down their heads to pray for a safe journey but surprisingly when we reached Adnemada everybody hurriedly left the bus without bowing their heads to thank God for having answered their prayers. I observed that they were like the ten lepers the Bible narrates that Jesus Christ healed, and out of the ten, only one returned to thank Him. I was interested in finding out whether these passengers were the same. I made up my mind that I was going to observe them at the Ednuoaya bus station. I tried to imagine how God functions but nothing reasonable came to my mind. It is really difficult to say anything definite about the ways of God. Seventy people will be in a bus, if an accident occurred and fifty-five died the fifteen left would each thank God for loving them and for saving their lives. What about the lives of the majority? Is it that God hated them? Truly the ways of God are not the ways of man. I concluded.

When the driver started driving the bus out of the park I threw a glance at the girl with whom I shared the same seat. She was the same girl I had admired earlier. She even looked more beautiful than then. I wondered if she ever went to the toilet.

'It would be interesting travelling with an angel' I said to myself as the driver negotiated the last bend leading to a road junction.

I noticed that she looked at me too and smiled beautifully in a way I had never seen a girl smiled before. Her smile was charming and reassuring, but it also reminded me of what my father had said about women.

At the main road junction, just in front of the bus station, there was a large crowd and many stationed vehicles. Our bus driver stopped the engine of the bus and went out to see what was happening. Within three minutes he returned with the news that an accident had occurred just in front of the regional hospital not far from where we were. He said that a young man had been killed by a heavy duty truck and that the boy's head was completely damaged beyond recognition.

'Dem di trai for si ha for adentifai de body. Dem dong see yi adentiti card and nayim dem go usam' he said. I felt disturbed that I had no national identity card.

'How would I be identified if something happened to me?' I thought to myself.

We got blocked in the traffic for over forty-five minutes before the road finally got cleared as the corpse of the victim was removed by the police and circulation resumed.

'What will be done to the driver?' Someone asked.

'Nothing.' Our bus driver said. He went on to say that from what he had gathered for the brief moment he went out, the boy was running across the road without looking and the driver who was not even at top speed tried to apply the brakes but it was already too late. One of the gendarme officers and other eyewitnesses were unanimous that the boy was on the wrong. 'He must have smoked those strong things they are fond of smoking.' An elderly man remarked and the topic was closed.

Everyone in our bus was happy when we finally drove out of town. We still had a long and tedious journey ahead of us. Those who were already used to such journeys and who knew how deplorable roads in this country are had their minds made up on what to expect but it was different with those of us who were travelling to Ednuoaya for the first time. The girl sitting next to me noticed that I was really nervous and asked me if it was my first time of travelling to Ednuoaya.

41

'Yes, it is my first time. I do not even know anyone there neither do I know where it is' I answered.

'How do you intend to cope there?' she asked again.

'My father's friend whom I've never even seen is there. He will have to pick me up at the bus station tomorrow morning. I know it won't be easy but it will only make me stronger. After all, my father says smooth sea does not make skilful sailors' I told her.

'Oh, that'll be okay then, I was already wondering how you were going to cope in a big city like that where you don't know any person. I live there with my elder sister and her husband who works in the ministry of Finance' she said and went on to ask why I was going to Ednuoaya. I told her my reason and she stated to me that it was difficult for one who did not understand French at all to cope in the University of Ednuoaya 1. However, she observed that my case could be different since I was going to enrol in the English Department.

'I am a second year Law student studying in the University of Ednuoaya 2' she told me.

'That's interesting. Are the two universities close to each other' I tried to inquire and she said they aren't that close.

'The University of Ednuoaya 1 is located in a quarter called Aonga. That is why some people refer to it as the University of Aonga while the University of Ednuoaya 2 where I school is in a quarter known as Aosa. The University is also identified with the name of the quarter. So if someone talks of the Universities of Ednuoaya 1 and 2 just know that they are talking of the Universities of Aonga and Aosa respectively' she explained. I told her my name and asked her what hers was. 'I'm called Gladys, but my friends call me *Lady G* for short' she said.

'Girls! Always trying to modify everything,' I said to myself thinking of a lady I had seen earlier that day whose name was Diane but she called herself Diamond. They are always exceptional in everything they do. From their long fingernails, to the over ten kilograms of mesh that they carry on their heads, to the layers of paints of different colours that they apply on their bodies...

Gladys and I discussed for some time before we eventually ran short of topics. She told me she wanted to be a lawyer and after a second thought, she added that she could be anything if she wanted because her elder sister was married to a worker in the ministry of finance who had a friend who knew someone who knew someone who knew another person who was related to the Prime Minister himself. I thought of what she had said and it didn't make much sense to me. She was giving me the impression that there was no merit in this country which I knew wasn't true. From her explanation, it looked like for one to succeed, he needed to know someone who knew someone who knew someone who was related to the political submit. I remembered the day our principal had dismissed his own son from school for slapping a classmate which was against the school rules and regulations. Those are the type of people we need in this country. I am sure that if that man is the minister of transport and his son doesn't do well in a driving test, he would fail. This country is rotten.

However, I thanked her so much and acknowledged that I was learning a lot about the town already. I also knew within me that my entire journey wasn't going to be as boring as I had thought. We stayed quiet for some time and eventually fell asleep.

'Bam, wake up' Gladys said waking me up from sleep.

We had arrived at the first checkpoint and everyone was supposed to step down from the bus and show their national identity cards to the gendarme officers who stood with guns as if they had been told that the person weaving a coup d'état to oust the God-ordained president of the republic was in our bus. My heart missed a beat when I saw the seriousness with which documents were checked. The driver had earlier asked me to stay in the bus and that was what I did. He stepped out of the bus and spoke to one of the officers. They spoke in French after which our driver extended a closed fist towards the officer who turned to the opposite direction

43

before extending his hand to collect the money from behind. I understood what it meant – the driver was giving bribe on my behalf. I felt guilty because I had always known that bribery is the enemy of justice! A feeling of guilt haunted me as I wondered if that was my own contribution to bettering this country. The officer moved close to our bus and stood by the door and pointed his long gun towards me. I couldn't believe I had come that far to be killed for not having a national identity card. I cursed the thief who had seized my bag. The officer only stood there for a few moments and left, then life came back to me and I felt that the front part of my trousers had become wet. I couldn't hold it any longer. My bladder had become loose and I had to hurry out of the bus through the back door. The driver noticed me stepping down and came to me.

'Na weti?' He asked.

'Piss dey do me' I told him trying to stop it from coming out again by bringing my legs together and dancing. He noticed that I was really pressed and pointed to a nearby bush just about a metre away. I stood there and relieved myself and he guarded me back into the bus. I was lucky the other officers never saw me. The driver also stepped into the bus and drove me pass the checkpoint before stopping for the other passengers to climb in.

From that point of our journey, the road was too bumpy that no one could have slept. We all stayed up with everyone holding tight to whatever they could as the bus went in and out of potholes and gutters.

'After over fifty years of independence, this is all this country can boast of as a road' one of the passengers commented.

'My brother, they all want to stay in power yet they can't construct roads in this country. We have no future. The worst thing is that they are doing everything to ensure that no Anglophone ever becomes president in this country' a second person observed.

'All Anglophones and some reasonable Francophones are fed up with the system in this country. How can you imagine that in the history of this country, fifty years after gaining independence from

44

France and Britain, we are not able to boast of our own currency? Isn't it really ridiculous that we are still using a currency imposed on us by the French government? We still pay colonial dues to France through this French currency we use called *france*. As if that is not enough, we also do so by saving our money in French banks dotted all over this country. How then is this country independent? Look at our neighbouring countries such as Airegina that gained independence at the same time with us. How I wish Anglophones had stayed there! They have their own money and that is reflected in the rate at which their economy is booming. But this country, the giant of Africa, uses money that bears the name of another country, France. Is France the only country that colonised us? Why don't we use Britain? I think the British were better in their policies. I swear to whatever you believe in that one day this will come to an end because the children of this land shall …' he was too angry at this point that though his mouth was opened no word came out.

His argument was having an effect on me. I sent my hand into my pocket and took out the money that had been contributed and given to me. I wanted to see if what he was saying was true. I saw *france* written in italics on the 1,000 note I was holding. I thought of throwing the money through the window but changed my mind. I took out the coins to check if that was the case with it and behold the same thing was written on them.

'My brother, leave it there' a fourth speaker began. 'Has it never bothered you that in close to fifty years this country has had only a couple of presidents? Is it that only two women were blessed since the creation of this country to be able to give birth to children who will rule us? Let me tell you people, by human nature we are bound to favour people we are familiar with such as church members, family members, tribesmen, friends and schoolmates. This is the reason we see that President Aybia Lapua's close collaborators are either of the same age range with him or from the same part of the country or attend the same church. I am not absolutely against that policy because as head you have to appoint those you know and can trust. It becomes disturbing when you are the head of everything – head of the armed forces, number one farmer, and number one sport man, head of the government, number one teacher, and number one looter of the national treasury. At the same time, we should know that the rotation of power will obviously bring a lot of positive change in this country. If Mr X becomes president for a single term of office and favours Mrs O, P, Q, R and S after him Mr or Miss Y can also become president and favour others. By so doing development will spread and people will not complain a lot. The problem is that a certain group of people have completely held the country hostage. We must understand that the sun will forever shine on those who stand before it shines on those who kneel under them. We have knelt under them for too long and have only complained in hiding. We have been made dogs that eat only bones, yet we do nothing about it. Even dogs do not actually prefer bones to meat; it is just that no one ever gives them meat' he ended.

'But must we, like the dogs, accept the bones?' another person asked.

'My brother, a dog which refuses a bone is not alive,' someone spoke from behind.

'Those of us from Adnemada have no choice', a fresh voice said. 'When they take all the important positions in the country and give us useless positions, what do you expect us to do? We can only patch with them as underdogs. Nooremaca People's Progressive Party for Change (N.P.P.P.C) has taken this country hostage. For about forty years, the N.P.P.P.C, through their fraudulent means, has always won in elections. Even before elections are done, everyone usually knows who will win and when the results are declared after a couple of months even those who set up the mechanism for fraud pretentiously appear to be surprised at the outcome. No one, except the N.P.P.P.C itself, is ever surprised about the victory. The other political parties just bow, because they've greedily compromised their desire to free this country from this dungeon and are now patronizing with the corrupt government. I mean ALL without any exemption! One would have expected Exhumed Sanitizers Deemed Fit (E.S.D.F) and Leaders in Alliance with Christ (L.A.C) to be different. NO! They all collect their crumbs and stay quiet, deceiving people from our side of the country and giving them false hopes.'

'We as a people in this country must rise against the injustices of our government,' the first speaker observed. 'The Anglophones must rise as a people in this country and not continue to occupy the position of second class citizens in their own *land of promise*. We have lived in fear all these years. If you fear something you give it power over you. Even those of our brothers and sisters who have been bought over shall one day realise that the beautiful things of this world have caused them to sell their own people. It is in the nature of man to look up to the sky and see the beauty of the moon, the sun and stars and immediately forget the fact that the same sky has a threatening thunder and striking lightning...'

'We can do nothing,' another person said

'We only have to be patient; patience is the mother of a beautiful child,' a woman said. 'To run is not to arrive. We have to be patient and wait for what the gods are preparing for us. Do we not say that when the gods cook we do not see smoke? Let them stay there and do what they want, we only have to remind ourselves that there is no medicine against old age and that death is a garment we all have to wear one day' she ended.

I listened to them speak and was frightened by what my country had become. When they eventually stopped speaking, I again thought of John Nkemngong Nkengasong's protagonist, Ngwe, in *Across the Mongolo* whose dream had been to one day become the president of his country, the Republic of Kamangola.

'Thank God I do not want to ever become the president of any country. I only want to be president of my own life, not even president of my family meeting. I do not want to ever rule over any person. I won't even want to be a minister in one of the uncountable useless ministries in this country' I thought to myself.

I have always been fascinated by the fact that there were more ministries in this country than there are people. Why should this country have the Ministries of Basic Education, Secondary

47

Education, Intermediary Education, Higher Education, and the Ministry of Vocational Training? Why can't these ministries be merged to a single ministry? It's even worse with the ministries of Development in a country that has not recorded any development in the past forty years. We have the Ministries of Local Development, Urban Development, National Development and Developmental Development. Can you imagine?

Gladys noticed that I was in deep thought and asked me what the problem was. When I told her what I was thinking of she said I was limiting my dreams and wasting time thinking about things I couldn't change about the system to which I responded that I was just being realistic and truthful to myself. Two gentlemen sitting directly behind us were having a serious discussion on the same subject but their focus was on the country's system of education. They were totally dissatisfied about every aspect of it.

'We can never make any remarkable progress in this country, in fact – in Africa with this transplanted system of education,' one of them – a teacher from the way he spoke, explained. 'We've copied everything from the red man without taking into account our own realities and specificities. Africans are very intelligent but the system of our education has rendered us unproductive. Everything in the school curriculum is practically theoretical and no serious practical work is ever done. Children are taught things at school that will never be useful to this country.

For example, of what use is it to this country for a pupil to spend an entire term mastering how to draw and label a butterfly? This is the only country in which if children are to be taught about how a television screen can be made, many theoretical lessons will be given to them on aspects that were not even important to the person who made a TV screen. The teacher will give over ten definitions of what a screen is and will go ahead to state and explain different types of screens, give dates, names of people and places rather than simply providing the material needed for the experiment and leading them in doing it. I bet you that children in villages in

48

this country who have never even seen a computer can give better definitions to a computer than the person who invented the computer ever thought of. Of what use is that to us? How does it help this country for students to have to spend sleepless nights memorising how to draw a map showing fishing off the coast of Norway? Is anyone in Norway studying fishing in Nooremaca?'

The system is completely void of a vision for the future generation. I talk as if those at the top know that there is a future generation in this country. When we were in primary school we were taught the names of top government officials in this country and hope was given to us that we were the future, *the leaders of tomorrow* as our teachers would say then. Today, I teach my pupils the same names that I was taught and tell them the same things I was told. The only difference is that someone who was minister of agriculture during my primary school days could be minister of public health today and someone who was Mvodo Idrissou then could be Idrissou Mvodo now. I don't know who they are deceiving' he ended. His friend immediately took the floor to express his own opinion on the situation.

'You're completely right, my brother. One of the major problems we have in this continent is the way we have completely imbibed the ideas of the red man. When they came to Africa we took them for our gods and the situation hasn't gotten better over the years. The black man has failed to realise that the red man keeps the real things to himself and hands down chaffs to him. The two things they used and still use even today to keep us in perpetual darkness are religion and education. The worst thing they did here in Africa was to take away our self esteem through slavery and we started thinking we were inferior beings. I can remember a song we used to sing in primary school that Africa was a dark continent. Europe, America and other parts of the world are quite developed in infrastructure; but I swear to you by any deity you worship and believe in, that the red man remains the most morally primitive creature on earth. They're so uncivilised to the extent that they still look down on other races. When they came to Africa, they made us believe that the solution to all problems lies in prayers and in churches but back in their countries; they teach their children that the solution to all problems lies in hard work and scientific innovation. How can you explain the fact that there are more churches here in Africa than in every other continent on earth yet we have more problems than all the other continents? Let me draw your attention to the fact that if there is an outbreak of any global disease on earth today such as the ones we've had in the past, the red men will rush to their laboratories to get scientific solutions while we blacks will rush from one church to another seeking for spiritual solutions. That is the mentality they have built in us over the years. Do you know that when the red man came to Africa he changed the African system of administration by appointing and installing to power those people who were loyal to him? It is ridiculous to hear the same red man laugh at Africa today saying there is no democracy in Africa as if they were democratic in choosing those rulers in the colonial era. It's the foundation they laid here. We are where we are because of the red man and unless the black man overcomes greed and regains self esteem, he will never come out of the despicable political, social and economic situation in which he now finds himself. The black man can be compared to a person whose car, as a result of shortage of petrol ceases in front of a petrol station and he stands there praying in tongues for God Almighty to send a solution to a problem he can solve.' He observed.

I enjoyed and learned from their frank discussion though I didn't completely agree with everything they were saying. The discussions about the injustices in this country went wild in the bus with many passengers expressing their opinions over the issue. No one was supporting the government which surprised me because the ruling party always had a landslide victory even in our own part of the country. How come no one in our bus was speaking for the regime?

Most of what they said was true. Those in power have decided to hold on to it forever. As the saying goes, *In the beginning it was so and so shall it be.* They are born and born again in order to remain officially young though physically we see that they are as

50

good as being dead. When is tomorrow? They keep saying youths are leaders of tomorrow? When shall that tomorrow come? Every Ednuoayan is born again. An average Ednuoayan is born at least twice, that is why we see corpses ruling us. Physically, they are old but their documents show that they are youths. If we go by what is documented, we can only conclude that Ednuoaya has the highest youth employment rate in the world. Our leaders are forever young!

I felt an urge to write down something. There was a pen in my pocket, I took it out and begged for a piece of paper from Gladys and wrote down my thoughts in a poem I tentatively titled, *Another Term*.

Another Term

Oh, Africa!

For how long will this happen?

Constitutions are altered to suit them,

To satisfy their egoism.

And now, a term of office is elastic;

Longer than life expectancy in this continent.

Those whom death has forgotten

Stay in office for scores unlimited.

A child is born

He grows and to school goes.

Names of leaders of his country he is taught.

And taught that tomorrow he'll become one.

If cholera, malaria, AIDS, Ebola –

Other viruses and poverty do not kill him

He grows into a man

And begs from those who led before his birth,

He is given crumbs.

And these vipers!

These venomous snakes!

They keep asking for new terms of office.

And another term

And another term

And another term.

Don't they have shame?

Can no African leader learn?

They were in power before Obama's birth.

He became president,

And now his terms are over.

His terms; shorter than a term here!

Can they not learn from Mandela?

Gladys asked to see what I had written and I showed her. She looked through the paper and smiled.

'You are quite creative and will make a good writer in future,' she said. I thanked her and collected the draft, folded it and slotted into my pocket.

We went pass two other checkpoints without me encountering any difficulties. It was at the last check point, just at the entry to Ednuoaya town, that things became extremely complicated. Checking was thorough and the driver found it difficult negotiating on my behalf. One of the officers, noticing that I had no national identity card, ordered me to lie in a pool of muddy water. He spoke in French and the only thing that made me speculate that that was what he meant was that he pointed to the pool. Other culprits from other buses were already rolling in it. I joined them and not long afterwards a woman who sat behind me in the bus was also asked to join us in the pool. Unlike me, she had her national identity card but it had expired. The officers refused to believe her when she explained that she had not even noticed it before. Her card had been issued on 5th October, 2003 and we were on 7th October, 2013. Its validity was expired for two days. Did they want her to produce a valid national identity card on the spot? The right thing would have been for them to advise her to procure a new one but all they wanted was to intimidate and torture her and in the end still collect bribe. She was asked to join the rest of us for a bathe in the pool of mud.

'What is the use of a national identity card? Isn't it to identify people in case there is a problem like that of the accident victim we heard before leaving Adnemada? Can an expired card not serve that purpose?' One of those next to me was murmuring when an officer judged that he was condemning them and gave him a heavy kick on the shin of his left leg. He fell into the mud and rolled in pain.

The old woman ended up paying 13,000france for carrying an expired card. I couldn't understand how the gendarme officers at the previous three checkpoints had not noticed the woman's problem. I doubted if they could even read and write. Some of them can't even read their names. They are officers thanks to the disorder and chaos caused by this evil regime in this country. Once you are related to someone who is related to someone who is related to someone who is related to the minister of defence you could become an officer of the law if you wanted to.

One of the gendarmes swore that I was going nowhere unless I provided an identification document. He said he suspected I was a spy or a rebel against the regime. The driver and some passengers tried to explain to him that I was a student and that my bag had been seized from me at the park in Adnemada with my card and some money in it but the he vehemently refused to change his mind. He even refused to collect the 2,000france bribe the driver was offering and insisted that I give the sum of 20,000france because my case was too bad. I even asked if I could open my travelling bag and show them my Nooremaca General Certificate of Education (N.G.C.E) certificates which were the only possessions I had on earth, one of them said I was insulting them that they had not gone to school.

I knew that that was my end. There was no hope of me leaving the place as all attempts made so far to get me out of it proved futile. I could now only count on the efficacy of the driver's acquaintance with one of the potbelly gendarme officers. His Pidgin was quite good, in fact, better than the driver's and I suspected he was an Anglophone. The driver discussed with him for over fifteen minutes after which he beckoned one of his colleagues to join them. They spoke again for over five minutes and when I saw the driver extend a closed fist to the second officer I knew he was buying my entry to heaven – my entry to where I was expected to undergo a metamorphosis, my entry to where I knew I could study and achieve my dream of becoming a university lecturer.

He asked me to get up and go into the bus. I got up, looked at my clothes and saw that my whole body was a mess. I was as dirty as Pa Ubia's pig. The elderly woman had not rolled on the mud. She only sat on the margin of the pool which wasn't as muddy as the centre where I was pushed to. I tried to clean it as best as I could but my efforts were in vain as the mud was much on me and the water with which I used to clean it was also very dirty.

It was already 8:25am and many passengers were visibly tired because the journey had been tedious all through. The traffic that blocked us right in Adnemada town, the numerous checkpoints where passengers were asked to step down and walk a distance of approximately five hundred metres pass the control officers before entering the bus again, the deplorable state of the roads and now this humiliation. Most of the passengers could no longer resist expressing disappointment on our late arrival to Ednuoaya. When I got back into the bus I had to stand for the rest of the journey. I couldn't sit to stain the bus seats or dirty pretty Gladys who equally sympathized with the predicament that had befallen me.

'Bam, don't feel so bad about your situation because in about fifteen minutes we will be at the bus station' Gladys told me.

Seventeen minutes after she told me that we were close to our destination, I raised my head thinking of asking her if we had not reached just when I saw some carvings on a notice board that attracted my attention. They read:

SAFE JOURNEYS VOYAGES,

ISSAMIYEBA PARK

EDNUOAYA

I was excited that we had reached our destination. The first thing that came to my mind was to call the uncle whose number my father had given me. Something crossed my mind and I shivered with fear. Did I still have the number? Was the number not in the bag the thief seized back in Adnemada? I didn't want to believe the games my mind was beginning to play with me. I tried to ignore my thoughts but they kept bugging me. The tired driver gradually slowed down the car and entered the park on reverse gear. All passengers scrambled to step down from the bus. One didn't need any special attention to notice that no one bothered to thank God for the journey mercies we had all asked for at the start of the journey. I was anxious to get out of the bus in order to check the number in my pockets.

There was no other piece of paper in my pocket except the one on which I had written the poem. I carried my hands on my head and stood like a statue confused on what next to do. I can't say whether I was standing on my feet because I couldn't feel them anymore. They were no longer a part of my body. What brought me back to life was Gladys' angelic voice.

'Bam, are you okay? Why do you have that look on your face?' I heard her ask.

I didn't know where to begin from, whether to cry, laugh, ignore her or explain the reality of my situation. Other passengers were already moving out of the bus station towards different directions. When I explained to Gladys, she advised me to stay at the park and wait for my benefactor.

'Your host will wait for your call, it's true. But if in the end he doesn't receive a call from you, it will just be normal for him to pass around this bus station and check on you since you already told him which agency you were travelling by' she explained. I felt that there was still an iota of hope. There was still some light at the end of the tunnel. I went to the bus carriage and collected my bag, the only property I had on earth. When I opened it, it wasn't to check for the number but to see if my certificates were intact and if I actually had clothes to change the muddy rags I was now wearing. However, I was a believer in the power of miracles. I thought that by some divine design I could see the number in that bag. In the end I saw nothing.

Gladys stayed back with me for thirty minutes before leaving.

'I'll have to leave now,' she said. 'Let's hope that your host come sooner or later.' Before leaving, she gave me a number to call. It was the number of their home fixed phone.

***

Chapter Five

***

That morning Timchia, the person who was supposed to host Bam in Ednuoaya was so worried and restless that the boy had not called. He knew that all was not well and that he needed to do something about the situation. He called back the number Bam had used in calling him the previous day but the person who answered said it was a callbox number and that he couldn't remember who and who had used his phone. There was no way to contact Bam's family since he never knew anyone who had a phone and who could get him speak to Bo Bam. He discussed the matter with his wife who was even more worried that someone her husband promised to help might have had a problem on his way to Ednuoaya.

Before going to work he passed through the park to check on the boy but he wasn't there. From the inquiries he made, someone told him that a couple of buses were still on the way and were expected to arrive not long from then. He was assured that no accident had occurred on Adnemada – Ednuoaya road, which was his greatest fear. He looked at his watch and it was already 7:00am. At that time, the bus in which Bam was travelling had not reached the park. It had been stopped and delayed at the checkpoint.

Timchia wondered what might have caused the delay. Was there a breakdown? Why has the boy not called? Could it be that they were involved in an accident? With the road's deplorable condition, he couldn't leave that possibility out.

He was a chief accountant in the Ministry of Finance. He knew how strict his boss was and recalled that he needed to be in the office at exactly 7:30. He decided he wasn't going to wait. He would go to the office and if the boy eventually called he could call back his wife to go and pick him up from the bus station.

At 11:00am he still didn't receive any call from Bam. He was beginning to give up about the boy. He felt so worried that he had to call Juliette, his wife, to suggest that she go to the bus station and check on the boy. His wife didn't know the boy she was going to check on but her husband insisted that she just go and loiter around to see if she could see any stranded boy. She could even ask from the agency authorities if they had any knowledge of a boy who was travelling to Ednuoaya for his first time and who had to wait at the bus stop for someone to pick him up from there. The woman accepted to go to the bus station in order to check on Bam. However, she informed her husband that she had to take a shower before leaving the house since she had waited for too long and had decided to begin her cooking. He had finished speaking with his wife and placed his phone on his office table when it rang. He looked and it was a strange number.

'Finally the boy is calling' he said.

He made up his mind to answer the call and ask the boy to describe his outfit and tell him to wait for his wife to come and take him. After taking this decision, he pressed the green button and listened.

'Alloooh' a deep sad voice of an elderly man spoke from the other side.

'Yes, who is on the line, please?' he said and listened again.

'It's Bo Bam. I am calling to tell you not to expect the boy again. We just received information that he was killed in an accident in Adnemada town. The boy didn't even leave Adnemada, he was crossing the road last evening when a big car knocked him down and he died on the spot' he said.

'That can't be! How come? He called me yesterday evening and told me he had paid his bus ticket. My wife and I have been waiting for his call since morning and I have just called her now to go to the bus station and check if he arrived and maybe had some complications' he said.

'No need for her going to check again. We have just received the brown handbag he left with and his national identity card and your number in it. We are expecting the corpse this evening which will be buried immediately because according to the reports we have received, his entire face was damaged beyond recognition. The corpse cannot be kept for long. My enemies have succeeded in destroying the pillar on which I leaned,' he lamented.

'It's difficult for me to believe this. How can a boy I spoke to yesterday suddenly die? And from all indications he might have died immediately after that call,' he speculated.

From the other side he could hear Bo Bam groaning and mourning the way men do when they are terribly hit by a predicament.

'I trekked down to Gnodnufa Three Corners where I could get a phone and network to inform you,' Bo Bam said. 'I also needed to send to the Adnemada Regional Hospital Mortuary the clothes the corpse will have to be dressed in. I have already sent them and will now go back up to see how far the digging of the grave has gone,' he added.

'Has someone gone to identify the corpse?' Timchia asked.

'Yes, my younger brother has just left for Adnemada. I sent him with the clothes because I am too weak to go that far,' he said.

There was some prolonged silence after which the two men said goodbye to each other and when Timchia was certain that Bo Bam had dropped the call he immediately called his wife to inform her of what had happened to the boy he was asking her to go and check on. After dialling the wife's number, he listened as it rang. When the wife picked, she was the one who spoke first.

'Yes sweetheart, I am almost done dressing and will be on my way in less than five minutes,' she said.

'No need mom, the boy's father just called that he died in an accident last evening and that he didn't even leave Adnemada town. I'm heartbroken,' he explained.

'Dear, who are you talking about?' his wife asked assuming the husband was making a mistake about the information he was giving her. Could her husband have drunk beer that early morning that he was already drunk?

'I'm talking of Bam, the boy we were expecting this morning from my village. He has died' he emphasised.

His wife was shocked and found it difficult to believe that the boy she was dressing up to go and check on was dead. At the end of the call, she sat on their matrimonial bed wondering what the boy's family could possibly think about her husband. She remembered how one year after their wedding, when she couldn't get pregnant, her husband's family started accusing her of witchcraft. On the other hand, her own family accused her husband of sacrificing their unborn children in exchange for wealth and even advised her to dissolve the marriage. It was now three and a half years of marriage and God was yet to bless them with an issue but they were living a happy matrimonial life. However, she had the feeling that something was lacking in their home and that thing could only be their own kids. Nobody takes the issue of childlessness lying down in Africa. Getting married to most people means giving birth to a number of children. Sometimes she read from her husband's discussions that he really yearned to have a baby. She knew that if she didn't succeed in getting pregnant and giving birth to at least a child, sooner or later her husband would need a second wife for that. Even if he didn't want to do so, his family would pressurise him and in the end he would have to succumb. She prayed to God for that every day of her life believing that only He is the giver of children.

While these thought ran through Juliette's mind, her husband was restless in the office. He was unable to concentrate so he decided to obtain a short notice sick permission from his boss and rush home to have some rest and calm down from the trauma he was going through. Fortunately, he didn't complicate matters since Timchia was one of those workers who rarely obtained permission or stayed away from work. When he got home, he found his wife in their room crying. He consoled her and they lay on the bed for hours

60

without saying a word to each other; only enjoying the comfort and protection they could from the security of their hearts and arms.

Back in the village, all members of Bam's family and the entire quarter were in tears and preparations were being done to receive and bury the corpse. Most of the women who had been wailing seemed to have been observing a momentary break or merely respecting someone who had more reason to wail freely. Many were now sobbing but one loud voice could be heard. At the centre of the compound under the dwarf cypress, Na Bam sat wailing and recounting her tribulations while ignoring all attempts made by quarter women to hush her.

Oh! Finally, finally, my fears are confirmed!

My leopard hunter has been hunted,

He has been destroyed in a land far away for me to go

Nih, Ngam, Ndzi, why have you people allowed this to happen?

Why have you beckoned on this only one?

Who will cover my nakedness?

Why am I alive?

Let no one hush me,

Let no hole be dug in this compound to bury my own

For if that is done, you'll have to bury me alive first.

The one the gods sent to me in daylight is no more,

He has been stolen in darkness by men and women with horns,

I have no reason to live

My all-in-one is gone,

Taken away by witches and wizards.

The roof has been taken off my house

The rain is beating me

And the sun is heating me.

What am I living for?

Who does not know in this village that good things never come to me?

Yesterday, he was strong and healthy and hopeful

Today, he will be buried with a stone in hand

For leaving this earth without planting a seed.

Why?

Why?

Why me?

Why me?

The woman went on and on until the rest of the women eventually joined her again and the compound became alive once more with the music of wailing. The corpse was finally brought at 5:30pm but because of the severity of the damage the body had suffered in the accident, only Bam's father and a few men were allowed to see it before its burial. No woman was allowed to view the corpse. All appeals made by Nyindô Ngàm's wives and especially Bam's mother to see their son's corpse before it was buried, were turned down. In fact, they were simply ignored. The women cried like never before.

After observing some burial rites, the coffin was finally lowered into the grave. How women and children cried! Every person who knew the boy's industriousness and how important he was to his family was heartbroken. After the final layer of earth was put on the grave, most of the mourners started dispersing. It was already dark and there was practically nothing to eat or drink. Even if food had been prepared, who would have eaten? This was the type of death that completely took away mourners' appetite and left their mouths dry of saliva but their eyes wet with rivers of tears to shed. The only people who never failed to eat in such circumstances were the grave diggers. As they rounded off with the levelling of the grave, a basket of corn fufu, vegetables and a fowl were brought to them.

The grave was now completely covered. It was time for the male family members; especially Bam's brothers, cousins and nephews to pluck fowls over his grave. This was a ritual performed in the Huba land in order to mark the transition from life to death and ease the movement of the spirit of the dead to the land of the dead. This rite was never omitted in a burial in Huba. It was believed that any family that neglected such an important aspect of a burial ceremony would suffer more death of other family members in the future.

When those concerned had all come out with their fowls, their father stood there with some elders directing them on what to do. In fact it was their father who performed the rite first. He stood on the grave holding a life fowl on his left hand and spoke while plucking the feathers and throwing on the grave.

'Bam, it is me your father standing on your grave. In Huba we believe that children have to stay alive till they perform this ritual on their father's grave when he is gone, but here I am performing it on your grave. Since you have gone before me, this is your fowl that I pluck,' he pulled feathers from the fowl and threw on the grave before continuing.

'Take this message to Nih, Nsom and Ndzi who went before you. Ask them what they have seen in that land that they keep taking you people away from us. Tell them to take me instead because I am tired of burying children,' he concluded and gave way for the younger ones to perform the ritual. They stepped forward one after the other and did a similar thing but theirs was brief.

63

'Bam, I am Ngong, your brother and this is your fowl that I pluck,' the first person said and stepped aside.

The rest did same from the third person to the fifteenth. In the end, the fifteen fowls were slaughtered, roasted, chopped into little pieces and eaten with corn fufu. It was customary for the chicken to be served in hands and eaten on the spot. Taking it home was taking death to your home.

Mourning lasted for a week during which many sympathisers brought some gifts to greet the bereaved and sympathise with them. No one in the quarter went to farm during that period. Men brought life fowls, firewood and drinks while women brought cooked food, corn, beans, oil or corn flour. During this period, cooking was done every day to entertain visitors. On the fourth day of mourning, all close family members completely shaved the hair on their heads. The women, who were really touched by the death such as Bam's mothers and sisters, marked a line with *cam wood* powder on their heads from the forehead to the back.

***

Chapter Six

***

At 5:30pm, I was still stranded at Issamiyeba bus station. An hour after Gladys left, I had gone to a nearby callbox with the intention of calling her to inform her that no one had come to pick me up, but thinking of my father's advice and doctrine on women, I changed my mind.

'She was really beautiful and had been kind to me that morning' I thought.

The fact was that I didn't want to let her know I was desperate. My fear was that she could sympathise a lot with me and we may eventually get intimate. I wanted to end it at that level. We had travelled together and that had to end there. After taking that decision, I tore the paper on which the number was written and threw the pieces away.

Two hours after the incident, I became so hungry that I desperately needed something with which I could sustain myself. That was the first time I was feeling hungry in over twenty-four hours. A woman nearby was selling beans and something that looked like bread. It had the shape of the pestle we used in the village to pound coco yams. Many people ate it with relish. My mother's lessons on how to eat were unknown to these people. How could people eat while standing? You would see a man well dressed in black suit, white shirt and black tie carrying a bag on his back like a hunter in the quarter. A man you judged was supposed to be married and you would expect that before leaving his home, he ought to have eaten food decently prepared by his wives, but you soon realise that you were wrong in thinking so. He will buy that long microphone in the name of bread which the woman selling opened with her sharp finger nails – finger nails, not a knife – and loaded it with beans, pepper and carrots. And the man, probably a minister, teacher or even a lawyer will, like a journalist reporting from a battle field, move around biting and discussing with friends. He will even catch some grains of beans falling off the bread with his unwashed hands and throw into his mouth, eat on and chat with friends who were behaving no differently. It was not easy for me to imagine myself eating in that careless manner and in that place. This was more so because of the unhygienic condition of the environment. A couple of metres from where the woman selling sat, was an empty container one would expect civilised men and women to dispose refuse in but unfortunately, that wasn't the case because my brother and sisters found it easier depositing all types of dirt the ground rather than the can. The dirt had formed a very high mountain that one could stand on and touch the sky. Nothing was done the right way. Almost everyone had abandoned the markets stalls and was now exposing their wares on the road thereby narrowing it and causing traffic. Yet it was no one's concern to address the situation.

It was only when my stomach started speaking a language I could no longer understand that I decided to buy some of the poison to destroy my system with. I just needed anything that could fill my stomach for the time being till I got home. I speak as if I had a home to get to. I went to the woman, who at least could speak pidgin, and asked her to serve me which. She did and I sat on the edge of her bench and munched it. It was really difficult for me to eat because the bread was too dry and the crumbs kept dropping on my body. The beans didn't taste nice either but I had no alternative at that moment and more to that I needed to get used to the system. When I finished eating, I requested for water which she gave telling me that a sachet was 50france.

'Where on earth is water sold?' I asked myself.

The water didn't have any of the characteristics of good drinking water. It had a yellowish colour, tasted salty and produced a funny smell. I paid the woman her money and left the place wondering if that was how life would be in this jungle.

Many vehicles came and left the bus stop yet I didn't see the uncle who was supposed to pick me up from there. I didn't know how he looked like or how he was dressed but something kept telling me he was coming and to me, every decently dressed man was him. From time to time, I went close to people, whom I suspected were looking for a person to ask if it was me they were looking for. There was this particular man I saw and moved up to assuming that, everything being equal, he was a normal human being with human feelings like anyone in our part of the world. I cupped my hands the way it was done back home when greeting dignitaries and elderly persons bowed my head down and greeted.

'Good morning, Sir,' I said with a broad smile expecting him to smile back at me and respond to my greetings the way a civilised human being would. It was already after 4pm, I couldn't understand afterwards why I had greeted as though it was still in the morning.

He looked at me from head to toe before speaking back. *'Goot money c'est le nom de qui?'* he said frowning. I tried explaining in English that I arrived that morning from Adnemada and was stranded because the person who was supposed to come for me had not come and my bag had been snatched from me with host's number in it. The gentleman got so angry and started insulting me in French saying I was a thief. Many of the people who were selling around that place turned to my direction with questioning looks, suspecting me because I had been loitering there for quite some time. I had no option but to stay quiet since I couldn't speak French and didn't want to create a bad impression there as I guessed that that place could end up being my home for a night, a week, a month or even the rest of my life.

Before that day, I always heard of street children from people who had travelled. I remembered having seen a few in Ubia movies on Pa Ubia's television. Here I was, doing internship to become a professional street child. I couldn't believe that I had travelled all the way from Huba through Adnemada to become a street child in a foreign land.

After the encounter I had with the rude man, I didn't know what next to do except wait, wait, and keep waiting for my saviour. It didn't take long for the poorly prepared food and dirty water I had eaten and drunk to start having an effect on me. I felt sharp bites in my stomach and a sudden urge to visit a toilet. It was an attack of diarrhoea as I guessed. I ran round looking for a toilet but found none. Even the travel agency had no toilet. I asked a couple of people who spoke back to me in French seeming not to understand what I meant by toilet. It was already threatening to come out. I ran up and down but couldn't see even a bush to drop it in.

'This place is backward in many aspects, I swore to myself. 'How can a place be without a rest house? Back home it is different as every compound has at least a toilet and one didn't even need to beg before using. Who sent me to this place?' I cursed.

I knew that I was going to release the thing on my body; there was no doubt about that. I felt like the lid to my anus had been taken off and what was in my stomach was gradually but surely coming out. Hot tears started coming out from my eyes and sweat from my face. There were veins on my neck as a result of the efforts I was making to stop it from coming out and disgracing me in public. An idea came to my mind and I ran back to the woman from whom I had bought the refuse that was now disturbing me.

'Mammi ... Mammi ... toilet shit' I told her holding my buttocks with my left hand as if to block my anus from sending out whatever it was about to release.

'*Go fo motto pay tu hundere*' she managed to explain.

I understood what she was trying to say. There was a toilet at the agency and I needed to pay a sum of 200france before using it. I thanked her and made an attempt to leave but realised that I couldn't. There was no way to move again. Moving forward was not possible and moving backward was even worse. She noticed that I was really pressed but there was nothing more she could do. I tried to tighten it a little more, calculated my steps and ran back to the bus station. The woman working there looked at me and understood that there was an evil spirit in my stomach that needed to be sent out. My deliverance didn't require prophet T.T Balak's prayers or the services of any man of God, as they are called. The solution to all my problems on earth at that moment was a toilet.

'Allez-y comme ça *'*, the woman at the counter, whom I saw as a saviour, said pointing to the direction of the toilet.

Before reaching there, I was holding a 1,000france note in my hand. I just threw it at the person who was standing at the door to the toilet and went in. By the time I pulled down my trousers I noticed that my pants were already wet. No need to think about anything! I immediately sat on the toilet pot and as soon as I freed my bowels, the thing came out as if someone had opened a waste tank. I felt some fresh air blew pass me and I smiled not sure why I was smiling. I stayed in that *delivery room* for over ten minutes doing my thing. After all, I had given the man; or was it a woman I didn't even look, 1000france and if they thought I was taking too much time they were free to double the amount and deduct 400france instead of 200france. It was only after I had finished *shitting* that I noticed I hadn't collected toilet paper. No big deal. I removed my pants, which faeces had already stained, and used in cleaning my anus with, after which I dropped it in a basket that was standing just behind the toilet door with pieces of used toilet paper inside. When I came out I didn't see the person to whom I had given the money. The place was disserted but it was no longer a problem to me. There was a drum of water standing by the entrance which I had not even noticed before entering that *shrine*. I washed my hands and went for my bag.

Fortunately, my bag was still where I had dumped it before entering the toilet. I picked it up and wiped the dust on it. Many people knew what had happened to me and I could discern from their looks that they were chocking with laughter but were trying to suppress it. The more daring rascals and badly brought up ladies laughed outright and made comments.

'Petit anglo, tu as déjà motoh?' said one of the uncivilised guys laughing so loudly.

I didn't answer him. I couldn't have answered them. I needed to leave the place to where no one knew what I had gone through within those passed minutes.   Darkness was already taking over from daylight.

I remembered having heard someone stop a motorcycle and said in French that *cent france Carrefou Yamo*. I didn't even know where the place was or what people went there for but I decided to do same because I desperately needed to leave that vicinity where I was at the moment.   I moved a little farther from where the people making fun of me were and stood by the road side waiting for a motorcycle. I wasn't there for long when I saw one. The person on it saw me and slowed down pressing the motorcycle horn.

'Piiimmp piiimmpp' he hooted.

'One cent France Carrefou Yamo' I said raising my index finger to indicate 100 in case he didn't understand. The man stopped and asked me to climb. In less than four minutes I noticed that we were already there because he stopped the engine and looked at me indicating I should get down. I got down and paid him. About 100 metres from where I stood, I could see beautiful lights of different colours – green, red and yellow shining from a giant storey building. The place looked to me like a bar, a hotel or a night club as there were many people gathered around it.

In order to satisfy my curiosity, I moved to the place. In the open space, men and women sat around tables saturated with assorted drinks. They drank, smoked, ate beef and chatted happily. In front of the building, not far from where I was standing, were many girls with decorated faces. The lights were bright enough here and I could see that most of the girls had applied on their bodies an overdose of every other thing except dresses. The powder, the eye pencil and jaw pencil were quite visible. They looked like well decorated pieces of furniture. Some had rings on their noses and handcuff-like earrings on their ears. Almost all of them had very long multicoloured fingernails which made me wonder if they were mermaids or human beings. One of them came close to me, placed her hand on my chest, with her long fingernails touching my lips. I was frightened and visibly trembling.

'Mon Cheri, on part?' tu veux le wee'? je vais te bien donner. She blabbed. I pushed her hand away from my body and moved away telling her I was looking for someone but that wasn't enough to make her leave me in peace.

'Combien? ... Dit moi,' she insisted.

I became very angry at her for calling me *Combien*. I told her right there that my name was Bam and not *Combien* as she assumed. She understood that I was an Anglophone and spoke to me in a language that sounded like Pidgin, English or French – yes, any of those three or a mixture of both.

'You wan mbumbu me? I don a bon prie. All style,' she said.

It was then that I understood they were selling sex. It was important for me to do justice to nature by acknowledging that the girl who harassed me was exceptionally physically beautiful. She was endowed with the type of beauty that could bring back a dying man to life. The type of beauty that qualified her as wife for the gods, but that was tempting enough to make a priest of the gods lose his senses and taste of the gods' food and lose his power and protection because of it. She probably, remains the most physically beautiful girl I ever saw.

As I stood there admiring her, the little man in between my legs started nodding like a lizard. No, not a lizard, he ticked like the hand of a clock. From the shape and size of her buttocks, one would require a ladder to mount her. I realised that the temptation was getting too much for me and that if I continued standing there I could eventually fall prey, so I left the spot wondering what the world was turning into and how much *a dose of sex* could cost in that *market*.

On another part of the building, I saw three men drinking

71

together with six ladies. The men were decently dressed but the women were almost naked. Just like the girls I had just escaped from, their breasts and bellies were exposed probably to attract clients. What they wore in the name of skirts looked to me like a piece of handkerchief one of the bosses they were drinking with had torn and shared among them.

I stood there listening to their discussion but understood nothing because the image of the bad angel of a girl I had seen moments earlier refused to leave my mind. All my attempts to push it to the back of my mind were unsuccessful. I decided to sit in front of the night club, buy a bottle of top and drink while thinking of whether to return to my homeland the next morning or stay and die in a foreign land. Again I was unable to think of anything useful. For the whole of the time I sat there with a bottle of *vimto* in front of me, I kept thinking of the prostitute and how she had caressed me. In a conscious attempt to defeat the lust and push her out of my mind, I decided she was only Jezebel sent from the pit of hell to derail me. Certainly, this was the type of girl my father had instructed me to stay away from. After making up my mind to resist the temptation by all means, I wrote a poem about her:

Her Behind

Her behind is wonderfully superfluous;

Graciously designed with material sufficiency;

A structure, that mocks the girls with tiny endowments.

The contours of her behind are topographically designed

As were those of the beauteous Helen of Troy

Have you watched her walk?

It's graceful, comforting, tantalizing
And seductive in its flexibility.
Effortlessly, it incessantly sways
In a seesaw manner
From right to left
Like a springboard, it vibrates.
Her behind is bounteously superb.

And she uses it not to cure,
But to cunningly lure men.
And men like Pharaoh's soldiers
Get drown in her red sea
Of consuming fire.
Her behind is a booby trap.

Lord, forgive me my trespasses.
Lord, lead me not into this temptation.
Lord, prevent me from swimming
In this great lake of consuming fire.

***

Chapter Seven

Not long after I had folded the paper and put in my pocket, a tall man in black t-shirt tiptoed to where I was sitting and seized my bag from me and turned to escape. I remembered that the bag contained my entire life and that if he got away with it that would be the end of me.

'THIEF … THIEF … THIEF' I shouted so loud hoping that people would hear me and come to help me retrieve my bag. I couldn't also completely trust in the efficacy of my shouting so I needed to do something more than just that. The proper thing would've been to get up from where I was sitting and chase the thief.

'Yes, that was the right thing to do,' I told myself and got up immediately and struggled unsuccessfully to skip over the tables and catch him. I ended up falling down and hitting my head on one of the chairs.

It was then that I woke up from sleep. Realising that it was a dream, I thanked my ancestors while holding tight to my bag which served as a pillow for me on the table. I decided to open the bag and check once more for my national identity card – I might have just been dreaming that it was lost. When I opened the bag I found only my certificates and the rags I had taken along in the name of clothes. I smiled after seeing that all my belongings were there. The dream I had just had reminded me of another dream I once had while in Primary Three. In the dream I was playing football with my mates as my team's goalkeeper. The ball came to me and I caught it with both hands. I had been fighting back the urge to urinate for quite some time. Now that the ball was with me, I obtained permission and was allowed to step out of the playground in order to relieve myself. I unzipped my shots and took out my little pipe with which I had to connect the waist out of my system. For some seconds, I felt nice because it was warm as if I was bathing with warm water. The warmth did not last long as I soon started feeling some undesired wetness between my ties. I woke up from my grass mattress with a start and realised I had urinated on the bed and on my school shots which was the only pair of shots I had which at least didn't have windows behind and which could be worn to school. It was almost morning because the cocks were crowing in unison. Fortunately for me, as I thought then, there was a huge fire on the hearth; the type of fire prepared during the corn harvesting season in order to facilitate the drying of corn in the barn. I saw it as an opportunity to place my shots over the fire to dry off the urine. I got a stick and hung the shots on, then attached it to the small barn over the fireplace for the heat of the fire to treat it. Then I went back to bed. It was my mother who woke me up from that second sleep after she had smelt the burning of clothes. When I woke up I was sorry for what my most desired shots had become; the fire had consumed everything and only the waistband was left. I couldn't go to school for a whole week. It was only on the second week that my father, after beating me, gave me another pair of shots he had bought from the market that I resumed school.The music in the nightclub was booming and people were still enjoying themselves. I looked at my wrist watch and saw with disbelieve that the time was already 4:14am. I had spent my first night in Ednuoaya in a night club.

'So this is how my life has become?' I asked myself trying to feign a smile.

The reality of my predicament stood before me in black and white. Here I was, standing in the middle of nowhere, neither did I know anybody nor French and had lost both my saviour's number and my national identity card. It was now clear to me that what had happened two days back in Adnemada bus station hadn't been a dream. The Fear of what my future would be griped me but I managed to stifle my anxiety in order to stay focused and positive. My father always said that a good hunting dog could go on a hunt without its master and still succeed in catching game. I was a good dog determined to hunt without a master. I didn't know what to expect in the future but I made up my mind and swore that I was going to cope at the university with neither a helper nor where to live. Many people were leaving the night club while a few still stood around in pairs of two forming one shadow each. I decided to move away from the scene to a more comfortable place where I could relax and reflect on the direction my life was going to take from then onwards.

In a few moments, I was out of the place and standing where I had met the beautiful prostitute the night before. While still contemplating on which direction to take, I instinctively yawned covering my mouth with my left hand. The stench that greeted my nostrils was so unbearable that I couldn't believe it was coming from my mouth. It was then that I realised that I had neither taken a bathe nor brushed my teeth in the last two days. I needed water and a toothbrush or a chewing stick. Darkness was gradually succumbing to daylight and I only needed to hang around for some time for the day to completely break.

I finally succeeded in buying, from a nearby shop, three sachets of water – the type of water I had bought the previous day from the mother who sold bread and beans. My fear was that the diarrhoea I had suffered was as a result of the water I drank but I had no alternative. I didn't know whether there was any stream around or any bottled water and I didn't know French, which appeared to be the only language the people understood, with which I could inquire.

***

Throughout my primary school life, I didn't have a French teacher. When I thought of this, it reminded me of the discussion between the teacher and the other gentleman who sat behind me in the bus from Adnemada to Ednuoaya. I wondered why they complained so bitterly about the system of education in Nooremaca. I remembered the lies I was taught from the very first day I went to school. That morning, we were made to stand in lines at the assembly ground from Class One to Class Seven. Prayer was conducted, the national anthem of the republic of Nooremaca sung and instructions

76

dished out to us on how to compose ourselves in school. Morning Inspection was done and pupils with unkempt bodies and long fingernails pushed out from the lines for the Head Master to punish.

When the assembly activities were over, a song was intoned for us to sing and march to our classes. I listened to the song and tried to sing too. Different songs were introduced each week for those of us who were still new in school to learn. I always enjoyed most of the songs and when I returned home, I would sit in my mother's house and sing them. I can still remember the song that caused me to start doubting the quality of education they were giving to us. The song was:

I remember when I was a soldier

I remember when I was a soldier

I remember when I was a soldier

I remember when I was a soldier

Hippi yap yap hippi hippi yap yap

Hippi yap yap hippi hippi yap yap

Hippi yap yap hippi hippi yap yap

Hippi yap yap hippi hippi yap yap

Though the song was enjoyable and many pupils liked it so much, it didn't make sense to me because I could not remember ever being a soldier. The message then was out of context to me and when I think of it today I still have the same feeling. Sometimes I think concepts would have been easier to grasp if we were conceived and taught in our native languages rather than in the red man's languages. These foreign languages only helped in making education more difficult for us. After all, the red man's intention was never to make anything easy for the black man. He was out to assimilate and enslaved the black man and that is why he forced his language down our throats. Language is the perfect tool for coercion. The English language alone was difficult for us to assimilate. This contributed to our reluctance to learn another foreign language, French. Learning was undoubtedly easier in the mother tongue.

When I reflect today, I still cannot understand the magic through which I learnt how to read and write the little English I now know. Even when we eventually started learning how to read, some of my mates found it difficult reading anything written in capital letters. Some could read the word reading but would have a problem reading READING.

I remember an incident that occurred when we were in Primary Four. A bully classmate of ours was made the Head Boy. His name was Idiot Ndim and his duty was to control noise and write names of noisemakers whenever our teacher wasn't in class.

Many of our mates dreaded having their names written on the list because our teacher, Mr Waindim Anthony, never joked when it came to the crime of noise making and failure to do assignments. Idiot Ndim knew that he wasn't bright enough to spell names of those he would want to write. Consequently, he made two of us, which he assumed we could write well since we were fond of answering questions in class, his friends and even changed our positions in class so that we were now sitting on the same bench with him. Our duty was to help him spell names of pupils. We too didn't know how to spell most of our mates' names. We developed a strategy in which we had to move round the class stealing books of culprits and copying out their names for our Head Boy to include on the noisemakers' list.

One day our teacher gave us an exercise and went to the Headmaster's office. While I was on the other column secretly copying out other pupils' names to be included on the list of noisemakers, my friend with whom I had that task intentionally wrote out my name and handed to the blockheaded Head Boy who foolishly wrote it down on the list. It was only when our teacher came and read out the names that he realised what he had done. However, he couldn't admit that it was an error since that would mean that he was dull beyond comprehension. The entire class knew he could not spell but no one ever said it beyond a whisper for fear that he would send his spies to get their names and could even get them beaten at the end of the school day. A situation as the one he was now faced with could have given pupils ample proof of his foolishness. He insisted that I had been making noise and that he had written my name intentionally.

I was given seven strokes on the guava branch cane on my buttocks. I cried the whole day and at the end swore to myself that I was going to do all I could to revenge on him. I only needed to behave normally with him for some time so he could forget and assume that I had forgotten about it.

The day of my vengeance finally came after two weeks. There was a staff meeting and all the teachers where in the Headmaster's office. The school was so rowdy especially my class. My colleague in the task of stealing books and copying out names was not in class that day due to ill health. I knew I was the only person our Head Boy could rely on for names but I intentionally made it slow in order for him to get desperate about it for fear of what our teacher could do to him if he came and didn't have any pupils to punish after having heard the noise that was coming out from our class. True, Idiot couldn't read but I knew he could identify Idiot Ndim as his name. So, I wrote down six names with one of them being NDIM IDIOT instead of Idiot Ndim. My man copied and wrote it on his list exactly as I had written.

Our teacher eventually came back to class. He was so angry because we had virtually turned the class into a market. He asked for the list of noisemakers and my *friend* confidently handed to him the one we had prepared. He read out five of the names and had to break for a brief moment scrutinising the list. I alone knew what was happening.

'NDIM IDIOT?' He sounded.

'Present SAH.' My man answered not thinking the teacher wanted him to get the whip as usual.

'So you wrote your name too? And in capital letters!' The teacher observed. The man turned to look at me but I turned my face and looked at the opposite direction. The class saw the shock on the man's face and burst out laughing. Our teacher was still shocked and confused. Another classmate explained to him that the Head Boy was never the one writing the names and that he had surely fallen into his own trap. The teacher said he was deeply disappointed in him. He got him beaten and demoted. The entire class enjoyed the moment but I knew I had to pay after school. As soon as the bell went, I rocketed out of class and disappeared to our house. The following morning, the tension had died down but we never became close from that day.

From Class One to Six, I always had a book written at the back *French Language* but it was only when we were in Class Seven that someone came to teach us French. He would come to class every afternoon to teach and would speak alone till the end of the period. The language sounded very strange to us and we showed no interest in learning it. The teacher was in the school for only a couple of weeks and abandoned us again because we were so blank in French.

While in Government Secondary School Gnodnufa, a Francophone French Language teacher was sent to teach us French. The woman didn't even know *good morning* in English. She came to class the first day and sat on the first bench discussing only with the few students who knew some sentences in French. These were students who had relatives in francophone regions of the country such as Ednuoaya and who usually went there during long holidays. When she left that day, she only came again once and that was all. It was only in Form Three that we had another teacher for the subject.

***

The early morning sun was beginning to rise. I thought of what I would have been doing at that moment had I stayed in the village. I would certainly have been on my way to the farm to clear the small piece of land my mother intended to cultivate huckleberry on. I had planned to do so but got busy with preparations for my departure from the village that it completely escaped my mind.

'She will have to cajole my brothers for quite some time before they clear that small place for her,' I said to myself feeling sorry for her.

The rising sun looked so friendly that I concluded it was welcoming me to this odd world. I crossed to the other side of the road and walked towards a bush where I intended to hide and brush my teeth and wash my face. After walking for about two minutes I raised my head to look ahead of me to know if there was a pavement, a stone or anything I could sit on and take off my shoes before brushing. I was already feeling pain on my feet after being with shoes on for over forty-eight hours. Behold, I was surprised by what I saw before me.

'Where am I? Could it be that the University of Ednuoaya 1 is somewhere around this place' I asked myself with some rivers of excitement flowing within me.

Right before me was a big signpost bearing some odd but recognisable writings. Though I didn't understand French, something on the signpost completely took my attention. It was the writings on it. They were written in French and in bold letters but it was neither the bold nature of the letters nor the fact that they were written in capital letters that attracted me – it was the message. On it was the following inscriptions in dark bold capital letters:

REPULIQUE DU NOOREMACA

UNIVERSITE DE EDNUOAYA 1

The signpost stood at a road junction and on it was an arrow showing one of the roads which made it relatively easy for one to guess which of the roads could lead to where I was thinking. I

81

sat on a pavement and looked across the road I believed led to the university but I couldn't see very far because there was a sharp bend after which was a piece of grassland. It looked like a farm that had not been cleared for over two years.

'No big deal, when I finish I'll have to follow this way till I reach the university campus if it can ever be reached on foot,' I told myself. I was determined that even if it meant just seeing the university campus and returning to my homeland, then I was going to do just that. That would've been an achievement for me.

For about thirty minutes, I sat on that spot brushing my teeth and thinking of the possibilities and the impossibilities that awaited me. Without a national identity card, without the phone number that ought to have turned my life around, without a house to live in, without any knowledge of French with which I could communicate and without Gladys or any friend to help me, I knew I was completely finished. The decision I had early taken to throw away Gladys' number appeared so foolish to me now than ever before. I wondered if she was thinking about me and whether she was missing anything from our last meeting.

'What about my family? Maybe they're worried about me now. Maybe my father has called and has been told that I never arrived and they are worried. Maybe they sent someone to the agency to find out if I travelled ...' those ideas ran through my mind and I became worried about the people who cared about me. I had come a long way and there was no going back on my plans to struggle and succeed and make my family proud of me.

'They can go ahead and cry for me now but when I succeed they shall all dance for me' I promised myself.

My thoughts were interrupted by some university students who were marching to school that early morning. From their swift footsteps, I knew they were very good students who had plans of taking over this country in future. I envied and wished to be part of that dream. When I remembered the discussion between the gentlemen in the bus during my journey to Ednuoaya, I sympathized with the students fearing that the time for them to take over might never come. It seems the old will never hand over power to the young.

When the second group of students passed, I decided to follow them to wherever they were going. They didn't talk to me and I didn't talk to them either. I even doubted if they noticed me when they passed. They were walking so fast that I had to jog at some point in order to meet up with them. Not far from the junction, they took a shortcut and I followed them. It was just a path that meandered through farms down a small valley where a stream flew. A small bridge made of plank for people to cross on was in a very bad shape that all the students I was following went down the valley and crossed the stream with the help of the stones in it. The volume of water wasn't much and the large stones in it took away the risk of someone falling and facilitated crossing. I moved exactly as they did; going down the valley, stepping on the stones to cross the stream and moving up to the other side of the valley to come out in the main road again. In less than fifteen minutes from the junction they'd passed me, we were in the university campus. I knew it was the University of Ednuoaya 1 because I saw another signpost.

***

Chapter Eight

When I got into the University campus, I felt completely lost. It was as though I was in a different world altogether. Even though the environment looked so strange, there was nothing so special about it except that I was conscious of the fact that it was the University of Ednuoaya 1. It was made up of many buildings but the one that caught my attention most was the *glass house*. I tried to imagine what it was for and could only reach the conclusion that it was a mirror for lecturers. It was my first time of seeing a glass house and I remembered Mr L.C.M, my English Language teacher in G.H.S Huba, saying that *those who live in glass houses should not throw stones*. That was his favourite idiomatic expression which he used in all situations and it always made sense. If he wanted to beat a student and he or she complained that their finger was paining or that there was a boil growing on their buttocks, he would use the expression.

'Stay quiet and show me your buttocks. Don't you know that those who live in glass houses are not supposed to throw stones?' he would say. If a student reported that they could not copy notes because a classmate had stolen their pen, we would expect to hear the expression;

'You are too careless. Can't you take care of the things your parents buy for you? There are thieves in this class and you know it. Isn't it clear to you that those who live in glass houses should avoid throwing stones?' he would lament. If students failed in a test and requested for a catch-up test, we were sure to hear the same thing.

'Did I tell you to fail? Remember, those who live in glass houses should not throw stones' he would say and smile before continuing with his ever interesting lessons.

84

Despite the number of times Mr. L.C.M used this expression, I never imagined how a glass house looked like. I didn't even know one actually existed. Around the building was a fence made of barb wires and to the top of its main door was a signpost with everything on it written in French which I decided not to pay serious attention to. I observed the building for some time and before I realized myself, all the students I was following were gone. I concluded that I didn't need them any longer. I could move around the large school campus without anyone's assistance.

I left the place where I was standing and moved up to what I considered were the main buildings. After climbing pass a long stretch of stairs, I took my right and negotiated a bend leading to a dark corridor. When I came out of the other side of the corridor, I saw a large crowd of students in front of a building. I could recognise one of the students from the group of students I had followed from the junction. On the side they were standing, the building had three doors but none of them was open yet. In front of one of the doors was written SCOLARITE which I later found out was the admissions office of the university. Many of the students queuing up there had folders in their hands. I didn't speak to anyone. I stood at a distance and watched them for some time. It was already 9:00am and the offices were not yet open. I was anxious to observe what was happening but when the official didn't show up at 9:15am I decided to move around in order to have a better view of the campus and maybe locate my department.

Just above the SCOLARITE were other buildings. On the wall of one of the buildings was written: UNIVERSITE DE EDNUOAYA 1, FACULTE DES ARTS, LETTRES ET SCIENCES HUMAINES translated as UNIVERSITY OF EDNUOAYA 1, FACULTY OF ARTS, LETTERS AND SOCIAL SCIENCES. This was the department I left the village with the intention of getting registered in. The feeling was no longer the same but I couldn't figure out what had brought about the change. It was likely the fact that I had nowhere to live and nobody to support me.

85

Standing in front of the department were groups of university boys and girls chatting happily about their experiences and exploits. You could see university in their physical appearance; their assorted dressing, conspicuous hairstyles, language and the type of bags they carried along. When I looked at them, I had the feeling that they were more civilized and organised than the ones I had just passed at the admissions office. I do not know if it was just some sort of bias but I saw a marked difference in their dressing and composure. From their discussions I understood that registration had begun and that there were a series of documents required for one to seek admission into the university. They spoke of things such as certified photocopies of academic transcripts and certificates, birth certificates, pre-registration form, passport size photos, etc.

I placed my bag on a baluster and leaned on it thinking it was more secured to stand where people spoke the language I understood and hoped that someone who at least spoke English would come to my rescue. I was beginning to feel that the worms in my stomach were rioting for food but I was afraid of eating anything because of what had happened to me the previous day. I was rescued by a boy who came around selling *puff puff* and sugar. When I saw many of the English speaking boys and girls buying it I also decided to buy some for myself and have a bite. It wasn't bad since the taste was familiar. The only strange thing about it was that it was eaten with sugar. I ate four of the balls and went down to the school tap where I drank some water before returning to the position I had chosen to stand the whole day hoping that God will send an angel to rescue me.

Not long after I returned, I overheard a boy telling the other boy with whom he stood that the room he had paid for that academic year was too expensive for him to pay all through and that it was large enough to accommodate two people. His intention was to convince the other boy to move in with him so that they could share the rents.

'I would've loved to, but my younger sister will have to come and join me. That is why I also rented a bigger room than that of last year. I needed it for my sister and I'. The boy declined. When I was sure I'd heard them well, I made a secret prayer to God thanking Him for showing me the way. I remembered something my father had said in one of my meetings with him.

"Son, if you want to go quickly, go alone, if you want to go far, go with others."

I decided that I wanted to go far in my journey to the top and in my quest for knowledge in that civilised world. Slowly, I moved closer to them, greeted and they responded warmly. Where I could get money to contribute and pay for a house was not clear but I didn't want to miss the chance. Was I to use my fees in paying rents? What then could have been my reason for staying in that land?

'My name is Bam, I come from Huba and I am here to seek admission into the faculty of Arts in the Department of English precisely,' I told them.

'I am Chah James and a Level Two student of this department,' the one who needed a roommate said.

'My name is Wandje Ernest in the same department', the other friend said.

We shook hands and I joined them in their discussion. The first name sounded like a Huban name and I secretly wished that we came from the same village. Not long after I joined them, I narrated my ordeal to which they both showed some sympathy but I could discern some doubt and mistrust in Chah's look and voice.

At the end of the day we had become so used to each other that people would not believe we were meeting for the first time. They made me understand that they had already compiled their documents and submitted their admission files the previous week and had come to school just to get more familiar with the school premises for that academic year. It had taken them a whole week to complete the admission exercise. I completely trusted these two newly gotten friends to guide me through the admission procedure.

'The first step is to pay in a preregistration fee of 10,000france to the school account in *Banque Française* de Nooremaca. After that you will need to go to any documentation around campus and fill an online Preregistration Form. When the Preregistration Form is filled and printed out, you can then attach it to the certified photocopies of your Nooremaca General Certificate of Education (N.G.C.E) Ordinary and Advanced levels result slips or certificates and submit in the admissions office.

Chah James and Wandje Ernest took me to a branch of the bank which was not far from the school campus. While there, I realised, as my friends had earlier hinted me, that there was a crowd of students scrambling to pay their preregistration fee. Chah collected a form from one of the bank attendants and gave me to fill after which he directed me to stand in one of the queues. I stood there for over thirty minutes on the same spot. It was Wandje who noticed that some students were giving bribe to the security men and some officials and were being served through a window by the side of the building. He rushed to where I was standing and asked me to give him 11,000france and the form I had filled. When I gave him, he left and was back in less than five minutes with a receipt showing 10,000france. We left the place for a nearby documentation where I chose my courses and the form was printed out. The secretary asked me to pay 300france which I did and my friends and I left the place. Were it not for Chah's knowledge of French we would've spent several days struggling there and maybe ended up achieving nothing.

They took me to the admissions bloc for me to observe how things were done there. It was total disorder and those in charge of admission took this as an opportunity to exploit and insult students at will. If your documents were not properly arranged, an official would fling the file away and push the student out of the office. The student would pick their documents and rearrange them before standing on the line afresh. Only those who had extra financial offers to spare were properly served. If one gave extra money to one of them, whom I later understood were senior students, they would collect the documents and arrange, then get them stamped and one of the forms given back to the student in question.

When we left from the scene, Wandje took us to a nearby cafeteria and paid for our meals. I started having a sense of belonging and a feeling of love and security around them. Though the fear of what my family might be going through not knowing my whereabouts invaded my memory, I tried to push it off my mind in order to think of a more hopeful future at the university when I must have succeeded in sailing through the undergraduate, master and PhD levels.

The three of us went to Chah's room which wasn't very far from the university campus. We had to pass through the university volleyball court and go through a dark corridor that led to the main road. At the main road, we walked for two minutes and entered another corridor separating a bar and a documentation. Directly behind the bar was Chah's room. I wondered if one could study there with the noise that was characterised of bars, but I dared not ask lest he change his mind and decide he wasn't going to accommodate me in his room. As soon as he opened the door and went in, Wandje followed and I entered after them.

It didn't take me long to conclude that the room looked so empty and I presumed it was so due to the neat arrangement Chah had made in it and above all because it was really very big as he had said before. The conspicuous items in the room included: a bed, a table and table chair, a clothes stand, a gas cupboard and a radio set. The few books that were on the table were so neatly arranged that I judged Chah's orderliness from them. Attached to the wall above the table was a piece of paper with something written on it but I was too tired to read. I needed to pour water on my body and have a nap before anything else.

'I haven't slept or taken a bathe for many days now,' I said sitting on the table.

'It's okay, let me put water for you,' Chah said and picked up a black bucket which he filled with water. I opened my bag, took out the file in which my documents were and carefully placed on the table making sure I didn't displace any of Chah's property. He showed me where I took my bathe behind the room and when I returned, it was already dark and Chah told me that Wandje had left for his house saying we could only meet again on campus the next day after I must have had my admission documents certified. He sat on the bed while talking. After oiling my skin and wearing a fresh set of clothes, I sat on the chair facing him and we had an honest chat.

'Thank you, brother for accepting to share your room with me without even finding out where I come from,' I began.

He smiled, looked at the ceiling and said he was doing nothing special to me.

'My father always says it is good to help people, even people you don't know because you never can tell where your help will come from. I can't really say I trust you but I have made up my mind to give it a try. If you betray my trust even the gods will know that I did it with a clean heart,' he explained.

'Brother,' I said removing the 80,000france from my bag and placing on the table. 'It is a miracle that I am here now with you and I tell you, how I will succeed here is a mystery because this is all the money I have on earth. There are no hopes that I'll ever have any link again with my benefactor. I rely on hard work and I can assure you that if success depends on that, then we will succeed.'

'The major thing now is for you to gain admission in the university. Things will be easier for you to secure your admission because I have already gone through the procedure and now know what it entails. We have to get the documents certified tomorrow and we'll continue from there,' Chah said.

Our initial plan was that Chah and I would leave for the Divisional Officer's office the following morning to get my admission documents certified, but I thought I needed to remind him that I had no national identity card.

'The thief made away with my national identity card. I hope that won't disturb?' I asked. He thought for some time before speaking again and when he did his voice was low and slow.

'The D.O's office is in town and there are usually many gendarme and police officers around the place. I will have to go alone tomorrow morning and get the documents certified so that we secure your place in the faculty first. We can inquire about the procedure for procuring a new ID later on' he said.

I found it difficult to believe that someone could be so kind. I tried to hold my tears while thanking him but I couldn't control the sorrowful joy that was overflowing in me. He noticed my tears and was deeply touched too. We stayed quiet for a very long time then I decided to have a look at the writing on the paper I earlier saw on the wall. It was a poem by John Nkemngong Nkengasong titled *WAILING IN THE JUNGLE*. I started to read the poem but could only read up to the fourth stanza. The poem was an attack on unpatriotic politicians but when I started reading it, the first lines reminded me of the pain and silent cries my absence might have caused my family and the tears the thief caused me by seizing my handbag with the phone number in it. It read:

WAILING IN THE JUNGLE

Will no one listen to the silent cries

From shanties choked with the'offending

    Midnight breeze

The scythes of oppression whirling in the wind

And the venom of corruption searing

    In plebeian blood

It is a cataclysm of terror and misery

With slaves in tyrants' garbs

    Turned amuck

Turned rodents in the barns of fruitful
    Motherland
Will no one listen to them cry

No one listens to the tortured infant wail
No one bears its pitying mother's sigh
No one heeds to the farm-farer's groan
In this desolate jungle…

    When I reached that stage I was so touched that I couldn't continue. Although I was a victim of circumstances, I felt slightly guilty that I had abandoned my family and my absence was causing them pain. I convinced myself that I wasn't an infant and that I wasn't wailing but I thought of my dear mother and the pain she could be battling with now that I was gone and no one knew my whereabouts.

'Chah, this piece reminds me of many things about life and this country. Why is this poem important to you, brother?' Why have you posted it on the wall?' I asked but Chah didn't speak. I was about asking him those questions for the second time and even louder when I noticed that my man was already deep asleep. I prayed, put out the lights and climbed behind him where I lay and slept like a baby till the next morning.

***

Chapter Nine

The following morning, Chah woke me up from sleep. I was deeply asleep when I felt that someone was shaking me. 'Bam, wake up, the day is clean,' he said when I opened my eyes. 'Good morning, brother,' I greeted rubbing my eyes with the back of my left hand and getting out of bed. Chah was waking me up because he wanted us to go and draw water from a nearby well that we would use in doing our laundry that morning. The well wasn't too far from our room. It was just a five minute's walk through some dark corridors from our room. On our way, I seized the opportunity to observe the environment for the first time.

The way the houses were built was quite different from the way compounds are built back in Huba. The compound where he rented in was built in a rectangular shape with six doors leading to each bedroom. The building was separated from another building by a corridor. It was difficult to say whether it was one building or two separate buildings owned by different individuals. What distinguished one from the other were the colours of the paints used in painting the two houses. Our building was painted with yellow paint while the other was painted with green. There was no yard for children to play and for things to be dried in as was the case with our buildings back in Huba.

There were many people at the main road going about their morning routine which basically consisted of selling, buying and eating poorly prepared food by the roadside. I saw many men and women drinking pap from bottles, eating *akara*, munching bread and beans as if they had no homes or pots. Back in Huba, you will not see a responsible person eating by the road.

At the well, there was a black ten litre bucket with a long sisal rope tied to it. We used the bucket in drawing water from the well and filling the containers we had brought. Chah told me he was asked to pay the sum of 400france monthly for the treatment of water and maintenance of the well.

When we returned home that morning, Chah pulled out a large bucket from under the bed in which there were some food items such as rice, garri, beans, and dried bitter leaves. He opened it and took out the plastic paper in which rice was tied and measured out two and a half cups of white rice for us to cook.

'I always prepare a single cup whenever I am alone. Now that we are two of us I think two cups will do and if Wandje comes he will have a little to eat too' he said covering the bucket.

As I sat on the table picking out dirt from the rice, Chah rushed out and returned after about five minutes with an onion, some tomatoes, some green spices and two cubes of maggi. He came in when I was just finishing my own task of selecting bad grains from the rice. I sat and watched him complete the process. In less than no time, he chopped the onion, tomatoes and the green spices into a single plate. He fetched a matchbox, took out a matchstick, struck it and lit the gas on which he placed a pot and after about thirty seconds poured some groundnut oil into it. He allowed it to heat for a minute after which he added a table spoon of salt before emptying the plate of tomatoes and green spices into the pot. He then stirred it and covered the pot for about two minutes while he washed the rice. When he opened it, an inviting aroma hit all my senses. I felt like I was seeing, touching and tasting the food already. He stirred it again and poured the rice, stirred it for some time before adding water to it.

In less than forty-five minutes food was ready. Chah dished out his and asked me to serve myself. I looked at his plate to see what quantity I could serve without embarrassing myself for the first time. They say the first impression counts. I had to dish out my plate using the quantity in his plate as a gauge in order not to overdo it and make a fool of myself.

I remembered my meal times with my brothers and cousins when we were kids. All our mothers were fond of putting food for

94

all the children in a single bowl so that we could eat together. As my father always said, food is sacred and it is in sharing a meal together that a good bond among children is tightened. My brothers and I had always enjoyed eating together until another much older brother, Nsom, came to live with us. He was actually the son of the daughter of my mother's mother's elder sister. My younger ones and I dreaded having to eat with him from the same bowl because he ate too fast and had the habit of bullying us into giving him our meat. Whenever we were eating together, there was always a silent communication among us such that neither our mothers nor any other elderly person could have understood. Nsom had instructed us on how to compose ourselves during meals whenever we were eating from the same dish with him. It was in our own interest to religiously obey and follow his rules because if we didn't do so, we would have to receive severe beatings from him on our way to the farm, stream or at home whenever the elders were away.

Whenever food was served, we were expected to wait till he started eating first. If you sent your hand into the bowl before him you were in trouble. Although everyone had their piece of meat, you were not supposed to touch yours until he took it and had a bite. He told us that biting meat was the most appropriate way to mark it so that someone wouldn't take another person's piece of meat. It was therefore his responsibility, in his capacity as the eldest, to mark our pieces of meat. You were not expected to put vegetables into your mouth without Nsom nodding his approval. If you did, you were in trouble. If you showed him and his nod was a disapproving one, it meant that you had taken too much. You only had to reduce it and show him again and keep reducing and showing him till he indicated that it was okay for you to put into your mouth.

'The food may not be tasty but it will serve its purpose which is to fill the stomach'. Chah said bringing me back to consciousness.

'Between true friends, even water drunk together is sweet enough,' I told myself before carrying the first spoon to my mouth.

The food was delicious as I had expected. We sat and ate

in silence. I remembered that in no stage of the cooking had Chah tasted the food but everything in it was okay. His cooking was probably better than that of many girls especially my younger sisters who when cooking, they would taste a million times but in the end the food will still be tasteless. I smiled when I remembered that whenever Bih prepared food in the house she never ate when others were eating. She always complained that she had cooked and lost her appetite. How would one not lose their appetite when they fill rice in a plate a number of times just to taste for salt? I always thought that it was the tasting that filled her stomach and she couldn't eat again when the rest of the family was eating.

When we finished eating it was a few minutes to 8 o'clock. Chah took my documents; my birth certificate, my Nooremaca General Certificate of Education certificates – Ordinary and Advanced levels and told me he was going to get them certified. I wanted to go with him but he asked me to stay back home since I had no national identity card and it was risky to go to such a place without an identity card. I had no other option but to stay at home and remain grateful to his kind gesture and hopeful to God that something positive was going to come out of my miserable situation.

The photocopies of my Ordinary and Advanced Level certificates required a fiscal stamp each while that of the birth certificate required both a fiscal stamp and a communal stamp. A fiscal stamp cost 1,000france while the communal stamp cost 400france. Our calculation gave a total of 3,400france. Chah took the sum of 4,000france and left for the *3eme* **Divisional Office** where he intended to get the documents certified. He was to use 100france in photocopying the documents and 500francs was to serve as transport.

According to our arrangements last night, Wandje ought to have come to keep me company for Chah to go for the documents. Chah observed before leaving that it was strange Wandje had not come yet. However, he assured me that he trusted that he was on his way. I stayed alone and completed the poem I had started reading the previous night. I went through it over and over wondering whether

John Nkemngong Nkengasong's portrayal of oppression, corruption and tyranny were also applicable in my country and society.

**

About thirty minutes after Chah left the house, Wandje came to keep me company. I was very happy having him around because it was boring staying in a strange environment alone. We discussed briefly about school and he took me to politics. In that little room, I learnt a lot from him about the bribery, corruption, military brutality that were subjecting us, Anglophones, to being mere slaves in our country. I enjoyed his deep knowledge of world politics and African *bellytics*.

'I am sure you were already bored being alone. Sorry I delayed on my way to this place. I came across a scene I couldn't have passed without standing there to observe and get what the real issue was,' he explained when he entered.

'Thanks for coming. Before Chah left we were wondering what had kept you back' I said.

'I was held back at the university road junction down there by an incident. One of our lecturers, Professor Ngam Mbah who teaches African Literatures and Civilizations, was slapped by a gendarme officer and trust him, he retaliated immediately,' Wandje explained. I adjusted my buttocks on the bed and gave him my complete attention.

'How can a gendarme officer slap a university professor?' I asked as a hint for him to continue.

'You don't know what this country has become'. He began.

'Every negative thing is possible in Nooremaca especially here in Ednuoaya. Eyewitness reports that the gendarme officer stopped the professor and asked him in French to present his car documents which he brought out almost religiously and on giving spoke to the officer in English. The officer collected the documents and said he wasn't giving them back until he explained in French what he had just said. The professor continued speaking in English that he could not do so which annoyed the officer and he had to respond with a slap saying the professor was insulting him in his dialect. The professor stepped out of his car, caught the officer by the neck and threw him into a nearby gutter to the applause of the crowd. As the officer struggled to come out, he landed on him and gave him two blows on the face. It took two of the officer's colleagues to pull him from the gutter with mud all over him. Without asking any questions, they started punching the professor and struggling to handcuff him. It was only when a campus police of the university came out and whispered to one of the them that the person they were beating was a university professor, that they left after warning him.

"T'as ta chance aujourd'hui. Sale anglo,"

'They cussed and took their bleeding colleague away. The professor, also bleeding, went back into his car and someone picked his car documents from the gutter where the gendarme officer had dropped them and handed to him. He thanked the young man and drove away' Wandje stated.

'What will happen to the gendarme officer for molesting a university professor?' I inquired from him.

'Nothing, he will go home and lick his wounds like a dog. I think he understands this country even better that's why he acted the way he did. He knew that reporting the assault to the gendarme's boss was of no use so he decided to handle it his own way. This place is a jungle and Professor Ngam Mbah is one of those intellectuals who have understood that even their education does not protect them from the brutality of this regime. This is the only country on earth where the person occupying the post of the Minister of Youth Affairs is eighty-years old. Does that make sense to you? Which project can an eighty-two year old Minister of Youth Affairs realise for youths in this century? Women are also crying that the Minister of Women's Affairs is never a woman. How on earth will a man understand and fight for the plight of women the way a woman would? This country is rotten to the core. After all, the ordinary citizens of every country are always better than the government of that country. But of all the countries on earth, I think the situation in this country is the worst! Our politicians have murdered the future of many generations to come. This country is one of the top heavily indebted countries in the world, yet politicians are caught on daily basis with tons of money in their homes. In their homes, I say! How can an individual hold the destiny of a nation hostage? And one would expect that when they are caught they should be punished. Instead, they are called to other functions. They are promoted. Only those who are a threat to the president are ever locked up.'

'This is difficult to believe. How do you expect me to believe that a class seven leaver will slap a professor – a nation builder and go scot free?' I asked.

'Forget about that grammar and face the reality,' he went on. 'No one gives a damn here. With these francophones and their French-acquired culture, no one is safe. I blame the British for auctioning us to a French colony. History has not favoured us at all and we have refused to correct that historical mistake. You can be a magistrate or the Pope or whoever you want to be, they will still kick you with their iron boots and nothing will happen. Professor Ngam Mbah is fond of saying that the red man is the most uncivilized person on earth and that after the red man is the Nooremaca francophone. According to him, the red man is primitive and uncivilized for looking down on the black man while the francophone is backward and foolish for marginalising the Anglophone. They marginalise a people they once referred to as "our Anglophone brothers".

He says it is difficult to believe that in the twenty-first century the red man still looks down on the black man in the fields of sports, science and the rest. He questions the fact that no African football team has ever gone close to winning the FIFA World Cup but a European team made up of only Africans can easily win the same title. I think he is right. Look at the French national football team for example. How many blacks were in that team when it won the World Cup? Does it mean they can only play well when playing for France and not do so when playing for their homelands? After all, I can only conclude that professor Ngam Mbah is right when he says Africans should stop wasting their time in football because even FIFA stands for Football Isn't For Africa. Just look at the way blacks are killed in Europe and America! What crimes do they commit apart from being black?' he elaborated. I only stayed quiet and listened to someone who already had university exposure and probably knew better than I did. I remembered what Mr L.C.M used to say about being ignorant of something.

'He who knows nothing doubts nothing,' he would say and laugh loudly.

Though they made sense, many of the things Wandje was explaining were strange to me so I needn't doubt any of them because I was totally ignorant. I had to stay quiet and learn.

'Look at the field of medical science,' he went on. 'Professor Mbah Ngam is right in arguing that the invention of VANHIVAX was criticized and neglected simply because the idea came from a black man. They reject every idea that is African. The red man creates viruses in laboratories and sends them to Africa where he later sends aid in order to look like the god of Africa.

That is how they control our economies and some idiots say Africa is independent. What is political independence without economic independence? Is there any political independence even? How can one explain the fact that during every election in every African country you hear that the French and the Americans have sent observatory bodies to monitor the elections? Have you ever heard that any African country sent an observatory body to monitor French or American election? This is ridiculous! What do they come here to observe if not to manipulate the results in order to put the candidates they can control in power? They only keep a candidate that will open our borders for them to come in and out as they like taking along piles of our natural resources free of charge. The red man's heart is red and his intentions are evil.'

'Think of those African leaders such as M. Ifaddaga of Aibyla and R. Ebaguma of Ewbabmiza who tried to oppose neo-colonialism by keeping the red man out of decision-making in their respective

100

countries and propagating the agenda of a United States of Africa. How did they end up? The red man shaded all the good work they did for Africa and said they were dictators. Africans sheepishly believed the traitor, toppled their governments and today they suffer in the hands of the red men who now extract raw material from those countries without giving any compensation. On the other hand, the red man celebrates and forces us to celebrate those African leaders who have been cooperative to their evil plan of remaining as masters while the black man remains a slave in his own land. Look at how they praise N. Alednana of Htuosa Africa for not taking revenge on them after leaving prison and becoming the first black president of his country. The red man molested the black man for so many years and when he was given the opportunity to retaliate like Professor Mbah Ngam just did today he embraced the red man and today the situation in his country has not changed. Blacks are still trampled upon but he is celebrated and accorded a Nobel Peace Prize for betraying and selling the future of his people.'

'When they came to Africa, they enslaved and killed our great grandfathers and raped our great grandmothers, bought their lands with broken pieces of mirrors, gave them only what was no longer useful to them including the religion which they ended up blindfolding the black man with. A religion they themselves no longer practise.'

'When I came in, I noticed that you were reading John Nkemngong Nkemngasong's *Wailing in the Jungle*, weren't you?' he observed.

'Yes, I was. I started reading it yesterday but was too tired to complete it. It's only today that I've gone through it and have started seeing the poet's line of thought. I was wondering why Chah put up the poem on his wall,' I said.

'In our second semester of Level One last year, professor Mbah Ngam taught us the poem in a complementary course called LITTERATURE AFRICAINE ET SOCIETÉ COLONIALE during which he instructed us to each put a copy of it where we could see each morning before leaving our houses and where we could see each evening when we return so that it will prepare us for the hardship we have to face in this country. Just to show you the place of an Anglophone in this country, let me inform you that that course was taught by four lecturers. By text, two of the lecturers were supposed to teach in French while the other two teach in English but that wasn't the case. Three of the lecturers were purely francophones who knew nothing in English and Professor Mbah Ngam was the only Anglophone who went against all odds to teach in English. It was extremely difficult both for the Anglophone students and the professor because it was a mixed class and francophones who outnumbered Anglophones became so noisy whenever it was the English lecturer's lesson. There were several occasions where our francophone brothers and sisters hid the microphone and the lecturer had to manage with his natural voice in one of the biggest Amphis on the campus. Whenever he left and a francophone lecturer came, the microphone resurfaced from nowhere,' Wandje explained. Someone knocked at the door to our room and shifted the door blind. We were happy that Chah had returned from the Divisional Officer's office. The smile on his face was reassuring and I was certain that he had succeeded in getting the documents certified.

'Prepare let's go to the campus and submit your admission file,' Chah announced still standing at the door.

My discussion with Wandje ended at that level as I took a black pair of trousers from the wardrobe to put on. It was then that I realised that I hadn't even offered Wandje food. We had been carried away by the discussion that I totally forgot my Anglophone hospitality and generosity. However, it wasn't too late for me to make up.

'Wandje, we spoke for so long that I even forgot to offer you food,' I said.

'Never mind, this is my house and if I wanted to eat I would've checked the pot myself. Just dress up let's go,' he said. Within thirty minutes we were in the university campus. The crowd at the admissions office was as large as it had been the previous day. It took me just forty-five minutes under my friends' directives to go through. When I entered the office and presented my documents, the attendant looked at my name for some time and asked:

'Mbam, ça c'est quel genre de nom? Tu sort d'ou mon tip?' he said.

'Sorry Sir, I don't understand French,' I told him.

'Parle en Français. Je te parle en Français tu parles ton partua à qui?' he said again.

'Sir, I said I don't understand French. I speak English,' I insisted, praying within me and trying to avoid annoying him for fear that he could return my documents and send me out of his office.

'T' est Adnemada? Les Adnemada viennent faire quoi ici? Restez chez vous, On a crèe un université pour vous à Adnemada. Tu cherches quoi ici?' he asked.

I stayed mute and he looked through my documents again more thoroughly signing them and putting the university and date stamps on them. When he was through, he took out one of the two academic forms we had printed the previous day and to which my passport photos were attached and handed to me along with the originals of my certificates. He then assembled the photocopies and the other academic forms and stapled them together.

We left the place that day very happy that I had been registered into the University of Ednuoaya 1. It sounded interesting to me as I saw it as an open door for me to achieve bigger things in life. We went to Wandje's place where he offered us a drink each in a nearby bar. The three of us sat there sipping our drinks and it was fun all through that afternoon until late into the evening when we got the news that a thief had seized a red man's bag at the road junction and had disappeared into the crowd. The gendarmes were arresting almost every male who was around the area especially Anglophones as suspects.

***

103

Chapter Ten

Wandje suggested that since it was risky for me and Chah to return to our house that evening especially as I had no national identity card, it was better we spent the night with him and only leave the next morning when the tension would have died down. Just when we were sneaking out of the bar to Wandje's room, six gendarme officers surrounded us and asked us to follow them. We tried to escape but it was already too late and we had to be taken to the 8eme Gendarmerie Post where we spent the night with many other suspects who had been arrested that same evening in relation to the same crime and locked up without any interrogation.

The following morning, an officer came and asked us to present our national identity cards. Those who presented theirs were asked to leave. When Chah and Wandje presented theirs, one of the gendarme officers collected them and held separately from the others. He said that the two boys and three others including myself who had no national identity cards looked suspicious to him. Others were begging but I knew that that was the beginning of my end. I couldn't speak in French and had no money to bribe my way out of that place. Initially, I didn't understand why the officer had held back Chah and Wandje's national identity cards but asked the others who, from their dressing and hair, even looked more suspicious to me to go home. The two boys were pushed back into the cell to join the three of us who had no national identity cards. Five minutes afterwards five fierce looking officers came into the cell and handcuffed the five of us and, without saying a word to anybody, left again.

'We are finished,' I said aloud not knowing what to expect. Chah and Wandje were trembling too but couldn't think of anything or any way out. A different set of officers came in and instructed us all to sit on the flow with our backs to the wall and stretch out our legs. We did as ordered. Five stools were brought in for us to place our feet on which were chained together before what was to go down in my history as the first severe beatings of my life began. We were given twenty-five lashes each on our soles. Shouting, wailing and pleading was a waste of time as the officers turned deaf and if you tried to disturb them from conducting their most treasured exercise, they kicked you violently on any part of your body without any consideration. When they were through with the beating, the chains on our legs were removed but Chah, Wandje and I could not stand. The other two mates looked okay. I noticed that they were hardened criminals that even the officers there were familiar with. This could be judged from the way they interacted. Earlier that morning, one of them had sent an officer with some money to buy cigarette for them. When the cigarette was brought, they had smoked and blown the air to our faces. They looked to me like the people who ought to be in that cell not innocent students like me who had travelled all the way from Huba for the sake of knowledge just to end up being buried alive here. They discussed and laughed with ease as if nothing had happened to them.

'Why are they keeping you and me here even when we have our national identity cards?' Chah asked in tears and between sobs.

'They want us to bribe them first,' Wandje said.

'I don't think so. They allowed others to go without them giving any bribe. Why should they single us out?' Chah asked.

'You don't understand these people. Those they allowed to go are their francophone brothers. You and I including Bam are not,' Wandje explained.

They agreed that if they were called out of the cell again they would propose to buy their freedom with the sum of 10,000france each. The night we had spent together in the cell had not been too bad because I had been with my two friends and the excitement of me just gaining admission was still in me. I started imagining what it would be like if they left me alone there and went home. Tears started flowing down my cheeks without me noticing. It was when

Chah asked me to stop crying that I realised I had been crying. I tried to hold back the fear and pain but it was difficult.

Twenty minutes later, the door to our cell opened again and an officer, holding two cards, in his hand, read out two names from them. They were the names of my friends, Chah and Wandje. The two boys got up from where we sat and I got up with them not ready to let them go and leave me to die in that cell. They were the only people I knew in the world who could be helpful to me. When Chah saw the frustration and fear in me, he whispered into my ear that they would try to bribe their way out so as to go and prepare in order to come for me later. I went loose and cried like a baby.

While my friends were out, one of the inmates tried to explain to me in Pidgin that there was no need crying. He said he had been locked up severally and that crying does not help in the cell. The only solution was for a family member or a godfather to come and pay a huge sum of money for your freedom even if you were guilty. He said it was one of his gang members who had seized the red man's bag and that he wasn't going to say anything to the gendarme officers until his lawyer-uncle came to bail him out. The other inmate sounded confident too as though they were either brothers or colleagues. After some minutes, the door was opened again and I expected to see Chah and Wandje pushed back into the cell but it wasn't the case. Rather, the officer read out two names, Ondoa and Onana, from a piece of paper he was holding. My two mates stood up and bade me goodbye before leaving the room.

For the first time, I sat alone in that room and I can say now that it was at that moment that I fully understood the reality of my predicament. There was no one to whom I could speak and be understood. When everybody had left, I tried to explain to one of the officers that I was innocent and that they had instead freed the thieves but he got very angry because I was addressing him in English. I decided I wasn't going to say a word until Chah and Wandje come back for me as they had promised. There was no need speaking to a people who abhorred the English language the way the gendarme officers did.

For a week, I watched seven days sail pass and there was nothing I could do. Each day, an officer or two would come and take me out and try to question me about my family background but I would stay quiet. More inmates came and left but neither Chah nor Wandje showed up. I began to lose hope in my dream because there was no door that could lead me back to freedom. The authorities were prepared to present me to the world as the person who had robbed a superior human being from a superior race. I noticed this on the fourth day of my stay at the cell. The red man came there to actually see the thief that had stolen from him and, as reports said, I was refusing to confess. I was sitting on a corner of the cell facing two wild newly brought inmates when one of the gendarme officers on duty opened the cell and called me out. I thought my messiah had come and I was about to be liberated. Far from that! He escorted me outside with a gun pointed to my head and my hands chained behind me. When I reached the hall, it was then that I realised I had been wrong in thinking that I was going to be freed, they were taking me out to present to their colonial master as the person who had seized the bag of money he had brought from France to buy Africa with. The red man looked at me for some moments and asked the officers in French whether I was the one who had snatched his handbag. Without any waste of time, and with exaggerated confidence and certainty, the devils in red caps accepted that I was the thief. The Commandant swore that he was going to use me to set an example to my colleagues who were probably hanging on the street corners waiting for other victims. He told the red man that he had received calls to that effect from the Righteous President of the Republic of Nooremaca – *Le Chef d'etat lui même.*

As soon as they closed the door and walked away, a feeling of despair for the black man and that of hatred for the red man filled me! The same people who came to Africa and took away the black man's self-esteem and freedom, stole his identity, his culture, his land, his minerals, his name, his religion and his God. That evening, I was given the beatings of my life. Three officers took me to a different room where they unlocked the handcuffs and ordered me to stand by a pillar at the centre of the room. I stood there and was asked to put my hands round the pillar. I religiously obeyed and did as they said. One of them brought out a chain from under a table that stood unconcerned at the corner of the room and used it to chain my legs. He also cuffed my hands so that I stood as if I was embracing the pillar. They then brought out their whips and started beating me on my calves, buttocks, back and even head. I cried so loudly expecting my mother in the village to hear that they were about to kill her son in a foreign land. The hardened torturers were not moved by my tears. I pleaded with all my strength but they kept on beating me until I became so weak that I could no longer cry. If not for their shadows and the rising and falling of the whips I would have thought myself dead. In fact, I was dead already and only waited to be buried. Only then could the tale of life and death have ended for me. I think I am alive today simply because I refused to be buried.

When they eventually stopped and untied me from the pillar, my corpse just fell to the floor. I later regained consciousness and found myself in the cell without knowing how I had gone there. My back, legs and shoulders were bleeding profusely and the pain was unbearable. It was the pain that reassured me that I wasn't yet a corpse.

Two days later, I was still groaning in pain when they took me out again. I thought I was being taken to hospital or at least to somewhere where I could pour water on my body after over a week. When we entered the main hall an empty sheet of paper was placed before me and a pen given to me to sign. One of the officers indicated that I should sign on the bottom of the page which I did wishing that it was my dead warrant. I wanted to die and stop suffering for another person's crime.

From there I wasn't taken to the cell again. Two officers carrying guns climbed with me on the carriage of a green Toyota 4WD and we were driven out of the gendarmerie. For the first time in over a week I had the opportunity to see people going about their normal activities. Wherever people were gathered, especially when we were passing at the university junction, I peered with the hope of seeing either Chah or Wandje. We passed through the city and were going towards a direction where there were very few people and houses. I knew they were taking me to go and do some manual work in one of their farms. I was enjoying the scenery and the fresh air that consolingly blew away the pains from my wounds until the car negotiated a bend and hooted in front of a gate on which *EDNUOAYA CENTRAL PRISON* was written in bold.

'So this is where they are taking me to?' I thought to myself and smiled. The type of smile a man smiles after realising that the gods have failed to vindicate him from false witchcraft allegations. The smile one smiles when everything else has failed to prove him innocent and he is about to be buried alive for killing someone he has never met before.

When I came down from the car, it was like going down into a grave alive because fate had not treated me well and man had closed his eyes and covered his ears to my sorrow and cries. Two prison officers came and grabbed me by my shoulders. I was taken to an office where my name was registered in a black cover book and a bold marker used to write N. 511 on my t-shirt. From there I was led through a dark dirty smelling corridor at the end of which was a hall with TEMPLE NOIR written on the door. The handcuffs were removed from my hands and one of the officers opened the door of the hall for me to enter.

I looked into it and saw a crowd of men parked like sardine in tins.

***

Chapter Eleven

***

I will never forget that first day in the prison cell. TEMPLE NOIR, as it was called. When I was pushed in, I noticed that the only free space in the entire room was around the corner occupied by a very huge man with broad shoulders and large muscles. The person that stood closest to him had a piece of ceiling with which he was fanning him. The huge guy was lazily sitting with his legs spread out such that I immediately deduced that no one else was allowed to sit close to him. His physical appearance instilled fear in me. My body became hot, my armpits wet and my legs visibly shaking. Everyone in the room looked at me but no one spoke. My wish was that someone should speak so that I, at least, know where to go and what to do.

'True, I was born physically weak but mentally strong. So think of what to do, Bam' I told myself. The young man waving the piece of ceiling had N. 510 written on his shirt. I imagined that he must have been the convict that entered there just before me.

After thinking for a short while, I made up my mind on how to behave. I was not ready for any person's trouble. I summoned some courage and went straight to where the broad shouldered man was sitting trying as best as I could to avoid any eye contact with him. Though all eyes were directed towards me, everyone in the room was quiet. When I reached where he was sitting, I collected the piece of ceiling from the man who had all along been waving it up and down since I got into the room. He smiled and stepped aside for me to continue. That was how I negotiated a peaceful integration into the club.

I eventually realised that I enjoyed many little favours because the *Presi*, as the man was called, would sometimes give

110

me his leftover food and that because of my submissiveness I was never part of any morning labour and beatings. That was my job and comfort for two weeks until one day the door to our cell was opened and a prison officer came in and discussed with my boss in French, handed over a thick bundle of money to him and took me out of the cell.

At the yard, I was given a new shirt to put on, handcuffed and pushed into the back seat of a black car with translucent glasses. I almost thought that they were taking me to my freedom but something within me stopped me from thinking towards that direction – it reminded me that freedom was farfetched. I sat close to the officer who was already in the car and the one who had pushed me in joined us and I sat in the middle. The third officer sat on the driver's seat and drove the car out of the prison yard.

After what I considered was an hour's drive, we reached our destination where the handcuff was removed from my hands before I came down from the car. It was a nicely built compound with a black gate at the entrance of which was the Nooremaca national flag floating from a dwarf pool. In the yard were many masked security men dressed in black and carrying heavy guns. All they were doing was space to and fro speaking to no one.

I was led to an underground floor where every place was quiet and while there, I didn't feel like I was still on earth. It was completely a different world where our footsteps and my panting were amplified such that they sounded so loud in my ears. When I coughed, it echoed as if someone had hit a drum. We walked to the last room and one of the officers gently scratched the door and said in French that they had brought me. The officer was addressing the person *Monsieur le Premier*.

I tried so hard to guess what was happening but was unable to think of anything. The door opened and a potbelly man stood naked before us. I could not see his face because he was wearing a black mask. I looked keenly and from his height and shape I was convinced that it was one of the country's political figures whom I had seen on the television several times. Just I couldn't make out which particular one of them it was. Two of the officers stood at the corridor while the other pushed me in and closed the door.

The room looked like the cult sanctuaries we see in movies. It was decorated with black and red clothes and candles of different colours placed before a large mirror. Just looking at the nature of the room brought tears to my eyes, but I didn't cry because I knew crying was not going to help me. It wasn't yet clear to me what they wanted to do with me but I decided to let them sacrifice me to their god if at all that was their intention. Then pointing a gun to my head, the officer ordered me to take off my clothes. I did as he had ordered, almost religiously, while sweating profusely. I knew that refusing was tantamount to committing suicide because those people had no conscience.

For two hours, I endured the worst pain of my life. I felt like they were inserting a pestle into my anus. How I wailed but no one was moved by my wailing. I find it difficult to describe it because it brings back those horrible images to my mind. Please, let me stop here and not talk about the bleeding and the pain I felt after that when I was taken back to the cell and dumped there to die in agony. I have gone through a lot of torture and pain in the last seven years that I don't even want to talk about because it brings back the horror I …

***

That was how my dream of acquiring university education ended and I was sent to prison where I was buried alive for the past seven years and only got released three days ago thanks to the kindness of Barrister Gladys, the loving beautiful kind-hearted girl I had sat with on the same seat on that fateful night I was travelling to Ednouaya for my first time. She practically exhumed me and brought me back to the world of the living. What she has done to me makes me believe the truth of my grandmother's saying that to be without a friend is to be poor indeed. May the good she has done to me be returned to her children and children's children!

Two weeks ago we were clearing the prison yard when a black car drove through the gate into the yard and parked. Because of the splendour of the car, my mates and I knew it could be a rich man. As usual, we dropped our blond cutlasses and ran towards the car ready to beg from whoever was in it. Begging from visitors had become our major means of survival. Behold, an active charming looking lady with a familiar shape stepped out of it paying no attention to us at all. She looked like someone I knew but what made me confuse was the mask she wore that covered her mouth and nose. On her left hand was a green folder and after hastily closing and locking the car door, she greeted the officers on patrol and walked into the reception room. I noticed that two or three prison guards were also wearing masks on their faces but we were already used to seeing most of the armed men in there in masks that I hadn't thought there was anything peculiar about wearing a mask. The other prisoners, feeling so disappointed, went back to where we had been cleaning but I stood there for some time trying to recall where I might have met with the lady.

'Reprend ton travail,' one of the prison officials shouted at me.

I was about carrying myself back to where we were working when the lady in question came out of the reception room. I couldn't completely make out her face but something within told me that I knew her. Suddenly I felt as if a flash of lightning had passed through me bringing to my memory some long forgotten information about myself.

'Miss Gladys?' I called with an uncertain voice.

She turned, looked at me for a second or two but turned her face away and fumbled with her car key.

'Miss Gladys? I am Bam, the boy with whom you travelled from Adnemada some seven years ago. I am the one whose bag was seized at the park. When we arrived Issamiyeba bus stop I realised I had lost the contact of the person I was coming to meet. You left me at the bus station waiting for him to come. He never came. Please, I have been through a lot of pain here. Help me.' I lamented.

113

She had opened the door to her luxurious car and was about entering when I said the last sentence. She turned and looked at me again carefully, took off her spectacles and wiped her eyes.

'Bam? This can't be true! Where have you been all these years? What happened to you? Why didn't you call since that time? I waited for you to call and confirm that you were okay but you never did. What happened?' she asked without stopping to breath.

'Please, it's a long story.' I said with tears flowing down from my eyes.

'You don't look good at all.' She remarked.

I tried to speak again but no words came out of my mouth. She noticed the pain in me and asked me to stop crying. We stood there for what I estimated was five minutes with her right hand placed on my shoulder.

'I only came here to find out some information about a client of mine who was locked up a month ago and the wife has hired me to secure his release or at least make sure he is well treated so that he doesn't get infected by the corona virus in this deplorable place. I don't usually come here.' She said.

I eventually calmed down and she handed to me a sum of 5,000france before driving off after telling me she was to come the next day for us to discuss. At first, I felt hopeful, but when I thought of how Chah and Wandje had abandoned me, I started entertaining the fear that she might never return to rescue me.

The following day, she kept to her word. She was there at 1:00pm and asked to speak with me. We sat for three long hours and I narrated my story to her from the day we separated at the bus park to that very moment that I was speaking to her. She had to stay patient and try to calm me down by saying a consolatory word or two whenever I could no longer control my emotions. 'I will try my best to free you from here.' She promised at the end of our discussion and drove out of the prison premises.

For the next ten days, she visited the place almost every day trying to secure my release. I can't really say how she went about it, all I am sure of is that things changed completely from the day she met me in prison. Even the officers there started being a little kind to me. Three days ago, I was called to the office. When I entered, I saw Gladys sitting on a chair by the door.

'Congratulations! You are leaving this place today.' She announced to me as soon as I got in. The smile on her face was kind and broad.

'What did you say?' I asked, not sure if I heard her well.

'I said you are now free to go home. You were wrongly accused and imprisoned without any trial and without a stated prison term...' She was still speaking when I fell to her feet crying and thanking her.

'Stand up! Don't do that here,' she said.

I tried to compose myself but it was difficult. She was given some papers in a folder to sign. I was also shown a place to sign after which we entered Gladys' car and drove off to the hospital where a general medical check-up was conducted on me. On our way home she lectured me on the outbreak of the Corona virus that was threatening to bring the world to an end.

'The government has instituted the wearing of face masks in public places compulsory to all.' She told me at one point of the lecture.

'What happens to those who are seen in public places without wearing masks?' I asked for lack of anything better to say. My mind was not completely in the car: it was far off in the village where my father and loving mothers were, far off in the university where I ought to have earned for myself some university degrees by now, far off in the hotel where I had been taken to and desecrated, far off at Adnemada where a thief had snatched my handbag.

'How can I be free?' I heard myself asking. Gladys heard me too.

'You are free! Completely free like the birds in the sky. Do not be hard on yourself because physical freedom is not as important as the inner freedom. You have to avoid thinking of anything that happened in prison.' She preached. I decided to be quiescent. The silence was awkward and I guess that was why she pressed a button under the steering wheel and the car radio started speaking. The panellists were having a debate on the severity of the virus Gladys had talked to me about. Most of the speakers where praise singers to the Righteous President of the Republic of Nooremaca, *le Chef d'etat lui même*. Only one of them, a barrister, spoke in English but with the little French I learned from prison, I managed to get a few things the others were saying.

'Let us not be ungrateful,' he said. 'It is thanks to the president of this country that the virus has not yet killed us all. He is the father of the nation indeed. We can see the measures he has put in place in order to curb the spread of the virus in this country. He has ordered the halt of schools…'

'And houses of prayers but has kept drinking spots and markets opened.' Someone burst out ignoring protocol.

'Please barrister, let the minister have the floor,' the moderator said.

'And he also has the country,' the barrister said.

'Stay quiet let the minister speak,' another panellist vomited.

'I won't! Let's stop pretending. The government has failed woefully and let me tell you all that if this virus is really in this country as the conscienceless and politically assigned doctors claim, then calamity will befall us. People will die and bury themselves. How can we explain the fact that more developed countries complain of their lack of testing facilities but in this country cases of the virus are identified and confirmed by military officials on road checkpoints? What can you say about the government limiting the number of passengers to be carried in taxies to three whereas the force in charge of enforcing that law drive round town parked like sardine in the military trucks? How can you explain that those who check masks move around without masks yet they collect money from defaulters? Who are the real defaulters here? How serious are we in this country? We can't keep…'

We didn't take long at the hospital because she bribed two of the hospital officials to facilitate the procedure. When we left the hospital, she told me how bad the country had become and that it was difficult to completely stay clean from the corrupt nature of the country. From the hospital, we drove to her house where I had the opportunity to use a bathing shower for the first time in my miserable life. For once since my arrival in Ednuoaya I ate a well prepared meal. While I was bathing, she was in the kitchen cooking. In about an hour after I had finished she'd prepared for me the type of food human beings eat. The okra soup was so delicious that I swallowed two heavy loaves of corn fufu in no time. I decided that it was true that the person who has not travelled widely thinks his or her mother is the best cook. Gladys' cooking was exceptional.

I wanted her to take me to the university campus because I could only trace Chah's room from the campus but Barrister Gladys proposed that the right thing was for her to take me to where a new national identity card could be established for me. While there, the Commissioner of Police was very friendly with us and I enjoyed the security of being around Gladys. It took us about forty-five minutes to complete the procedure after which she paid some money and we left.

'The right thing for you to do now is to return home and see your family. Here you are alone in this world of chaos. You can't achieve anything alone. The elders say that a single stick may smoke, but it will not burn. You need to go home and unite with your family. Even little children know that if a man is in harmony with his family, that's success. Go home and see your family for they must be wondering what happened to you. A family tie is like a tree, it can bend but it cannot break. Your relationship with your family and ancestors has been tampered with! Go home and mend it. Return to your roots first because you can't succeed alone. Cross the river in the crowd and the crocodile won't eat you. Remember that Anglophones in this country are only mice in this Francophone injustice. You now have a taste of it, go and come for the real fight if you must. The mouse that makes jest of a cat has already seen a hole nearby. Do you have any hole you can hide in, Bam? I shall keep you at the park tomorrow to travel back to Adnemada and meet your family and decide whether you still want to go to school. If you still do, I will always be ready to assist you in my own little way.' She explained.

I wanted to tell her that one of the reasons for which I really needed to see Chah was because I needed my certificates but something stopped me from saying it. I wanted to ask if she was married but something stopped me from asking. I wanted to ask if she lived in that big house alone but something stopped me from doing so. What right did an ex-convict have to interrogate his redeemer? What if she got angry and sent me back to the prison, where I belonged by the judgement of the corrupt government of this country?

I only thanked her immensely telling her that she was a blessing in my life. She appreciated my gratefulness and asked me to go to bed. When I went into the room, I had to battle with insomnia for so many hours before succumbing to sleep. During the period that I was awake trying to forcefully invite sleep, my mind sailed into the activities of the day and I remembered that wherever we passed, people were panicking, washing hands, wearing face masks as a result of the outbreak of the recent pandemic called Corona virus. The news was full of stories about the plaque. Since I was unable to sleep, I decided to ponder over issues related to the virus. My ideas appeared in verse and even though I couldn't find a pen in the room to pen them on paper, I tried to memorise everything.

I WILL STAY A LITTLE LONGER

The race has reached its acme,

A plague has been unleashed from hell

Or from heaven if you like –

Or from a laboratory – some say

Death has lost respect –

For man, for fame, for position, for money –

Humankind scramble to die

The red man and the black man alike,
But I will stay a little longer and see the end.

The world has turned against itself,
No school, no jobs, no life, nothing.
And man has stopped progressing,
Life is either stagnating or regressing –
And we are encouraged to be lazy
To stay home and do nothing or die –
But I will stay a little longer and write a story

The TV and radio have no other news
It's all about Covid 19 –
The deaths – the figures – the lies
It looks like the world is ending
But I will stay a little longer and read a book.

I will stay a little longer and see my land of birth.
I will stay a little longer and...

  I cannot really say at what time I fell asleep that night. The following morning, she dropped me off at the bus station and gave me some money to come home. I was confused when I came into the compound and everybody was running away from me. I have gone through a lot in the last seven years that I don't even want to be reminded of. I ...I ... I ... I have ... only been ... exhumed thanks to Gladys.

***

"When he reached that stage, Bam started crying so convulsively that he couldn't compose himself to speak anymore. The men who had been listening looked at each other and dropped their heads almost at the same time. Nyindô Ngàm again thought of his last two encounters with *Bo finyha* and agreed to himself that what he had prophesied has come to pass. He felt guilty that at his age he still could not understand the ways of the gods or even respect their prophet. Bam's mother stood up and walked to where her son sat. She wanted to be sure that it wasn't just a dream. When she touched him, she felt that it was real and the emotions that were once buried in her rejuvenated as her heart bumped against her rib cage and she lay before her son wailing."

'I told them that my son was alive but no one listened to me. After all, I am just a woman who can make no observations in a man's world. I am only a woman whose duty is just to cook, clean and bear children for whom I cannot even take decisions. In the first place I was never in support of Bam going to the city but my opinion never meant anything. My son would have been married by now and living in his own house with his children. A thief was buried in the place of my son; I know I would have known from that corpse that he wasn't the one in that coffin.' Bam's mother lamented.

Chapter Twelve

'Stay quiet woman! This is not the time to apportion blames. The right thing to do is to go to your house and mobilize your mates to prepare something for my son to eat,' Nyindô Ngàm cut in. Bam had more than one reason for sympathizing with his mother. He had abandoned her for seven long years and now that he was back, her eyes were filled with tears. He thought that it would have been better he stayed on and died rather than return to cause pain to his loved ones for the second time. He wasn't happy the way his father had shouted at his mother. He thought of the African proverb that a mother is God number two and wondered why his God number two should go through all this pain. Timchia served himself a broad smile when he heard that food was to be prepared. 'Words are sweet but they never take the place of food,' he thought.

The other men in the house shook their heads, looked to the ceiling over their heads and raised their hands to appreciate God for bringing back their son to his land of birth. They were happy that finally their friend's son, whom they thought was dead and whose corpse they thought they had buried seven years ago, was back home and alive. Many of the people who had been outside all along and had been craning their necks in order to see Bam and hear him narrate the story of his journey to Ednuoaya and back were filled with amazement after hearing what he had gone through. As soon as he stopped speaking, the people, arms folded, formed pairs to discuss about the revelations of that morning.

While some were returning to their various homes, others stayed behind to make sure they completed what they had started. These were the type of people who eat food and lick the pot before leaving. They will always hear stories from the beginning to the end unlike some of the early leavers such as Dioma'a whose main reason of leaving early was to make sure those who were not at the scene heard the story from his mouth before hearing from any other person in the village. Dioma'a was the type of person who would only listen to a story and lie that he had been at the scene. He only needed to see the beginning of a confrontation and he would go round the village narrating from beginning to the end. That was exactly what he was going out to do.

Bam's mothers, being the domestic engineers that they were, got so busy in their different houses each, trying to prepare the best meal they could for their son to eat. Other quarter women joined them in preparing the food. During such rare moments, Nyindô Ngàm's wives knew that they were free to catch any of their husband's fowls and slaughter. The cooking was much and some of those who stayed back knew they were going to have a nice time there. It could only be compared to the feast ordered by the rich man in the bible to celebrate the homecoming of the prodigal son. Back in the house, Bam's father was addressing his son, feeling happy that their fears of having a ghost in their compound that morning and his fears of him dying and being buried just anyhow were almost completely conquered.

'Wonders, they say, shall never end! We are sorry, my son that we buried you alive. We regret to have buried you before your death. Don't cry, my son! Rain beats a leopard's skin but does not wash away the spots. Be the man that you've been these past seven years even in the grave and in jail. How could you have succeeded out there when we had performed funeral rites here in your name? Remember that every dog is a lion at his own gate and now that you are home, *Bo finyha* will clean the filth. He saw all these things and told me but I refused to believe him. Only he can guide us on how to get the solution to the problem we ignorantly created and I hope he exhumes and liberates you as he has promised to do. The world is wicked and the rulers of this country have connived with the red man to block our eyes as you say but the witchcraft of a stranger cannot be stronger than that of his host. It is from here that we tied you. We shall exhume you and let you go into that jungle and conquer it. Remember that you are a flea and that you can trouble a lion more than a lion can trouble you. When spider webs unite they can tie up a lion. You are now reunited with your people, your family and your land of birth. The wind that has shaken you cannot destroy you because wind does not break a tree that bends. You will be exhumed, my son.